TRADITIONAL GREEK HUSBANDS

Notorious Greek tycoons seek brides!

Childhood friends Neo and Zephyr worked
themselves up from the slums of Athens
and made their fortunes on Wall Street.

They fought hard for their freedom
and their fortune. Now, like brothers,
they rely only on one another.

Together they hold on to their Greek traditions…
and the time has come for them
to claim their brides!

Last month Neo's story:
The Shy Bride

This month meet Zephyr in
The Greek's Pregnant Lover

All about the author...
Lucy Monroe

Award-winning and bestselling author
LUCY MONROE sold her first book in September
2002 to Harlequin Presents®. That book represented
a dream that had been burning in her heart for
years—the dream to share her stories with readers
who love romance as much as she does. Since
then she has sold more than thirty books to three
publishers and hit national bestsellers lists in the
U.S. and England. But since selling that first book,
the reader letters she receives have touched her
most deeply. Her most important goal with every
book, is to touch a reader's heart, and when she
hears she's done that, it makes every night spent
writing into the wee hours of morning worth it.

She started reading Harlequin Presents novels very
young and discovered a heroic type of man between
the covers of those books—an honorable man,
capable of faithfulness and sacrifice for the people
he loves. Now married to what she terms her "alpha
male at the end of a book," Lucy believes there is a
lot more reality to the fantasy stories she writes than
most people give credit for. She believes in happy
endings that are really marvelous beginnings and
that's why she writes them. She hopes her books
help readers to believe a little, too...just as romance
did for her so many years ago.

She really does love to hear from readers and
responds to every e-mail. You can reach her by
e-mailing lucymonroe@lucymonroe.com.

Lucy Monroe

THE GREEK'S PREGNANT LOVER

TRADITIONAL
GREEK HUSBANDS

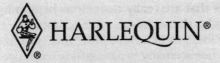

HARLEQUIN®

TORONTO • NEW YORK • LONDON
AMSTERDAM • PARIS • SYDNEY • HAMBURG
STOCKHOLM • ATHENS • TOKYO • MILAN • MADRID
PRAGUE • WARSAW • BUDAPEST • AUCKLAND

Recycling programs
for this product may
not exist in your area.

ISBN-13: 978-0-373-12935-5

THE GREEK'S PREGNANT LOVER

First North American Publication 2010.

Copyright © 2010 by Lucy Monroe.

THE GREEK'S
PREGNANT LOVER

For my beautiful daughter Sabrina, her wonderful husband, Kyle, and their precious child, Nevaeh. I love you all so much, and am so very, very, VERY proud of you. I thank God to have you as blessings in my life. Kyle and Sabrina, you have a love worth memorializing and you prove the truth that romance is more than fiction. I pray you are blessed for many years to come with as much or even more love and happiness as your dad and I share.

PROLOGUE

ZEPHYR NIKOS looked out over the Port of Seattle, remembering his arrival here with Neo Stamos over a decade before. Things had been very different then. Everything Zephyr owned fit in the single tattered duffel bag he'd carried. He still had that duffel bag stored in the back of his oversized walk-in closet, behind the designer suits and top-of-the-line workout gear.

It was a small reminder of where he had come from, and where he would never be again.

They had been so sure this was the place to start their new life, the one that would move them as far from the backstreets of Athens as a man could get. And they'd been right.

Two Greek boys from the wrong side of the tracks had built not just a business, but an empire worth billions of dollars. They dined in the finest restaurants, traveled by private jet and rubbed shoulders with the richest and most powerful people in the world. They'd realized their dreams and then some.

And now Neo was in love and getting married.

As much as everyone else saw Zephyr as more easygoing than Neo, *he* wasn't surprised his friend had found domestic bliss first. Zephyr wasn't sure he would ever find anything like it. In fact, he was near positive he wouldn't. Oh, he might marry someday, but it wouldn't be a hearts-and-flowers event, just another business transaction. Just like how he'd been conceived.

He had learned early that a smile made as effective a mask as a blank stare, but that's all it was…a mask.

His heart had turned to stone a long time ago, though he guarded that secret as well as he guarded all his others. Secrets he would never allow into the light of day.

Even Neo did not know the painful truth about Zephyr's past. His friend and business partner believed Zephyr had had a similar childhood to his own before they'd met in the orphanage at the age of ten. Neo could not imagine anything worse than his own messed-up childhood and Zephyr wanted to keep it that way. The pain and shame of his past had no place in the new life he'd built for himself.

Neo had hated the orphanage. However, once Zephyr accepted his mother was not coming back for him, it had been the first step in distancing himself from a life he wished he could forget. His father had thought nothing of selling Zephyr's mother's "favors" along with the other women who "worked" for him in the business that supplemented his less than stellar income from the family olive groves. And he cared nothing for the illegitimate son that had resulted from his own "sampling of the merchandise."

When Zephyr's mother had first left him at the orphanage so she could pursue a life away from his father's brothel, his innocent child self had been sure she would come back. He'd missed her and cried and prayed every day she would return. A few weeks later, she had. To visit. No matter how much that small boy had tearfully begged her to take him with her, she had once again left him behind.

It had taken him a few visits, but eventually, he'd realized he was no longer part of his mother's life. And she was no longer part of his. Which even a small boy, barely old enough to attend school, had been able to recognize as freedom from being a whore's son. An orphan, at least, had no past.

He'd learned to hide his. From everyone.

He would have stayed in the orphanage until he finished

school, but the monster whose blood tainted his own had decided an illegitimate son was better than no son at all. And Zephyr had had to leave. Now his best friend, Neo, had gone with him and they had made their own lives on the streets of Athens until lying about their ages to join a cargo ship's crew.

The move Neo considered their first step toward a new life, the life they now enjoyed. But Zephyr knew better. His journey had begun long before.

The simple truth was, as hardened as Neo appeared to be, inside—where it mattered—Zephyr was stone-cold marble in comparison.

CHAPTER ONE

"WHEN are we going to drop the bombs?"

Piper Madison's head snapped up at the question asked in a small boy's high-pitched tone. The dark-haired moppet, who could not be more than five, looked at the male flight attendant with earnest interest.

Glowing with embarrassed humor, his mother laughed softly. "He hasn't quite got the hang of not all planes being geared to war. His grandfather took him to an aeronautical museum and he fell in love with the B-52 bomber."

She turned to her son and explained for what was clearly not the first time that they were on a passenger plane going to visit Grandma and Grandpa. The little boy looked unconvinced until the first-class cabin flight attendant added his agreement to the mother's. Small shoulders drooped in disappointment and Piper had to stifle a chuckle.

There had been a time not so many years ago that her fondest hopes included being in that exasperated mother's place. Those dreams had died along with her marriage and she had accepted that. She had. Yet as much as she wished they didn't, those old hopes still caused a small pang in the region of her heart in moments like this.

But dreams of children definitely had no chance of resurrection in her current situation.

Trying to let the low-level background hum created by the

plane's engines soothe nerves already stretched taut, Piper leaned back in her seat and looked away from the domestic tableau.

It didn't work. Despite her best efforts, her heart rate increased as anticipation of her arrival in Athens thrummed through her. She couldn't stop herself looking out the window, her eyes eagerly seeking evidence of the airport.

For hours it had been nothing but a blanket of cloud with the occasional break where the peaks of the Alps crept through. It had been a while since she spotted the last peak and she knew they were almost to their Athens destination. Less than an hour from seeing *him*. Zephyr Nikos. Her current boss and part-time bed partner.

She was more than a little keen to see the man and the place of his birth. Besides, who didn't want to visit paradise?

For that's where they were ultimately headed, a small Greek island that at one time had been the vacation home of a fabulously wealthy Greek family. Not so flush now, the patriarch had sold the island to Stamos & Nikos Enterprises. Zephyr and his partner, Neo Stamos, planned to develop it as an all-inclusive spa resort. And she'd been given the interior design contract for the entire facility, with a budget large enough to bring in whatever kind of help she needed to see it to completion.

She was beyond excited about being brought in at the ground level on such an expansive project. It would be an amazing coup for her business, but satisfying personally on a creative level as well. Even so, her current heightened sense of anticipation was predominantly for the man who waited for her there.

She had spent the last six weeks missing Zephyr with an ache that scared her when she let herself think about it. She should not be so emotionally dependent on a man who was only *sort of* her lover.

She bit her lip on a sigh.

They were involved sexually, but not romantically. They weren't anything as simple as casual sex partners. That would be too easy. She'd know exactly how to handle her one-sided emotional entanglement then. But they were friends, too. Good friends. The kind of friends that hung out at least once a week before the sex benefits started and that increased to multiple times a week when they were in the same city.

To complicate things even more, he was also her boss.

Again…sort of. His company had hired her personal design firm for several projects over the past two-plus years, though this new development was by far the biggest and most far-reaching for her. He would be her boss in actual fact if she'd let him, too.

He'd offered her a staff job with salary and benefits she'd had a hard time turning down, but Piper had no desire to work for someone else. Not again. Not after losing both her husband and her job in one fell swoop only six months before she took on her first project with Zephyr's company.

She'd vowed then that she would not allow herself to ever be that vulnerable to upheaval again.

She'd thought marrying Arthur Bellingham would give her the stability she craved, among other things—like that family she'd dreamed about. It had turned out just the opposite, though. Art had shredded her emotions before tearing her life apart piece by piece until all she had left was her talent and her determination. She would never be in that place again.

Not even for Zephyr. Not that the sexy Greek real estate tycoon was offering her marriage, or even commitment. He'd offered her a salaried job. That was all.

If she wanted more, she certainly wasn't saying so. Up until the past weeks' long separation, she hadn't even admitted it to herself. Telling him wasn't in the cards she planned to play. Not when doing so would spell the immediate end to this whole friends-who-are-sexually-intimate situation.

And maybe their friendship as well.

Zephyr waited for Piper near the luggage carousel. He hadn't seen her in six weeks. She had been on a job in the

Midwest and he'd known if he didn't offer her the Greek job, he probably wouldn't see her again for another two months, or more.

Not that she wasn't the best interior designer for the job, but this project was bigger than anything she'd taken on before. He knew she could do it, though. And it wasn't as if he needed to explain his choice to anyone. That was one of the benefits to being the boss. The only person who might have something to say about it, and only because they were both working together on this development for the first time in years, was his best friend and business partner, Neo Stamos.

However, the man was knee-deep in wedding preparations right now. Cass might not want a big production, but Neo wanted their small wedding to be perfect in every way. Hell, Zephyr was surprised his friend hadn't insisted on designing and building a venue just for the event.

A group of newly arrived travelers surged toward the luggage carousel, bringing Zephyr's thoughts firmly to the present. He scanned the crowd for Piper's beautiful blond head. There she was, her attention caught by a small boy talking animatedly to his mother. The signature blue skirt-suit Piper wore highlighted her curves deliciously, while managing a claim to elegance. Yet, he doubted it was a designer label.

Piper's business was still operating on too fine a line for her to splurge on clothes, or even an apartment much bigger than a closet. He'd offered her a job that would have made it possible for her to live at a higher standard, but she'd turned him down. Twice. Damn, the woman was stubborn. And independent.

He wondered if she would turn down a shopping spree in Athens's fashion district?

She looked up and their gazes met. Eyes the color of a robin's egg filled with warmth and pleasure as they landed on him, her bow-shaped lips curved in a gorgeous smile. That look struck him like a blow to the chest.

He felt a grin take over his mouth without his permission,

a more honest smile than anything that usually masked his features. Not that he had to hide that he was pleased to see her. They'd hit it off when he hired her to update the main offices for Stamos & Nikos Enterprises a little over two years ago. Their friendship had only grown since. The addition of phenomenal sex to their relationship had only improved the situation as far as he was concerned.

In fact, Piper had been the reason Zephyr had encouraged Neo so strongly to develop interests outside their company, and to pursue his friendship with Cassandra Baker, the famous recluse master pianist. That had worked out better for Neo than Zephyr could have imagined. And Zephyr was happy for him. He really was.

However, it boggled his mind, to tell the truth. *Neo in love.* Zephyr shook his head. Sex and friendship were one thing, love something else altogether.

Piper's delicate brows drew together in a frown and she gave him a questioning look.

"It's nothing," he mouthed.

When she reached him, he pulled her into a tight hug. Her soft curves felt so good against him, the low-level arousal he'd experienced since waking that morning and realizing he would be seeing Piper today went critical. Just that fast.

Damn.

"I guess you *really* missed me." She leaned back, a sensual chuckle purring from her throat, her eyes glinting with teasing humor.

Chagrin washed over him. He wasn't some untried adolescent. Nevertheless, he laughed and admitted, "Yes."

"When is our first meeting with the architect?"

"The day after tomorrow."

"But you told me I needed to be here today."

"You needed a break."

"Building a new business is always consuming."

He shrugged because he couldn't disagree. For the first ten

years when he and Neo had been building their fortune, they had worked weekends and long hours during the week and hadn't taken so much as an afternoon off. Things had gotten a little better after that, though they were both too much of overachievers to develop much of a life outside their company.

After meeting Piper, Zephyr had started leaving the office around six instead of eight, but he still wasn't great about taking time off. However, Piper had sounded exhausted the last time they'd spoken on the phone, and he'd determined she would take a break, one way or another.

"Agreed, but I did not think you would begrudge an extra couple of days in Athens."

Her eyes lit up. "You mean I actually get to do some sight-seeing before submersing myself in the job?"

"Exactly. I'd hoped you'd consider the next couple of days as information-gathering time as well as our time on the island. We want the resort to fit into the island's ambiance, but also reflect Greek culture."

"Ambiance? I thought it was a private island. Empty."

"The family leased out land for a small fishing village and a few farms for local produce, as well as having their own fruit orchards and olive groves."

"Oh, that's perfect for what you are wanting to do."

"I thought so." But he enjoyed how in-tune with his vision she was.

"I'm glad I'll have time to really get to know the area then. I like to try and make my designs reflect the local setting's positive attributes."

"I know and I'm sure you've done a lot of research on Greek culture already." Heck, she'd researched it when they'd first met, telling him she wanted to understand him and Neo better as clients. He didn't know how much it had helped her, considering he and Neo had left Greece behind so many years ago. But there was no denying Piper *got him* in a way no one else did. And her design updates in their offices had been perfect. "Nothing can replace experiencing an environment in person though."

Unconsciously nestling her body into his, she smiled, clearly pleased. "True, but I didn't know I'd have the luxury to do so with this job."

He just grinned and shrugged.

She laughed. "Don't fool yourself into believing I'm not aware you have your own agenda here. One that includes judicious amounts of time between the sheets. You're a manipulator, you know that?"

She knew him well. "Is this a bad thing?"

"In this case?" She shook her head, her bright blue eyes going heavy-lidded. "No. Definitely no."

That's what he appreciated so much about her. Piper Madison was a gem among women, his very own polished diamond that did not require the setting of a relationship to shine. Unlike Neo's less worldly Cass, Piper had no illusions of love and romance. She enjoyed his body as he found pleasure in hers. No morass of untidy emotions to navigate, which was a very good thing.

Because unlike Neo, Zephyr had no love to give. "Let's get your case and we'll head to the hotel. It is a spa-resort."

"Scoping out the competition, are we?"

"Naturally." He gave in to the desire that had been riding him since her arrival and kissed her. And then he kissed her again for good measure. She tasted as sweet and arousing as always.

Eyes glowing with pleasure, she said, "Only, situated in the city, it can't hope to offer what we, I mean Stamos and Nikos Enterprises, will."

"There would be no point in developing a new property if we couldn't bring something to the table no one else has already offered."

Her azure gaze slid to his lips and stayed there for several seconds, and then she blinked at him with unfocused eyes before seeming to remember what he'd said and smiling wryly. "Always the overachiever."

"And you are not?"

"Hey, there's more than one reason you and I are such good friends."

"More than this, you mean." He rubbed himself against her subtly.

She gasped and stepped back. "You are dangerous." Letting her gaze drop to what he hoped his suit jacket hid from others' gazes, she winked. "I think getting to the hotel is a definite necessity."

"Are you tired?" he asked, tongue in cheek. "Need a lie down?"

"Get my case, Zephyr." She gave him a look that said she knew exactly what kind of lie down he had in mind and she wasn't necessarily averse.

"Gladly, *agapimenos*."

"Don't start in with the Greek endearments unless you want spontaneous combustion right here," she warned.

"But I like living on the edge."

She gave a significant look to the baggage rolling by on the carousel.

He turned smartly and started looking for the zebra-print luggage he had bought her after she complained about how her black suitcase looked like everyone else's in the airport. She'd laughed at the loud black-and-white print on the cases, but she used it.

She'd only brought one midsize case and her carry-on, so they were out of the airport and in the car he'd rented for the week a few minutes later.

"Mmm…nice. Definitely a step up from the Mercedes," she said, rubbing the leather upholstery in the fire-engine-red Ferrari convertible.

"Don't knock my car. It has heated seats and those come in handy in Seattle's colder winters. And a convertible would hardly be practical in such a wet city." But he was glad she liked the Ferrari. He'd wanted to spoil her a little, since she was always so determined not to spoil herself.

"There is that." She brushed her hand along the ceiling. "Are you going to lower the soft-top?"

"Of course." He pressed a button and the roof slowly disappeared.

Once the process had completed, he put the powerful car into gear and backed out of his VIP parking spot. With well-practiced movements in cutthroat driving, he maneuvered them through Athens toward their hotel. He swerved around a taxi that had stopped in a no-parking zone and then accelerated through a light turning red.

She put her head back and laughed out loud. "Oh, I like this. We really have two days for you and me to play, and nothing else?"

"We do."

"Thank you, Zephyr." She brushed a hand down his thigh.

Pleasure at both the touch and the gratitude he heard in her voice filled him. With an independent woman like Piper, it had been a risk to schedule vacation time for her without her knowledge. Even if he called it locale research. He was glad the risk had paid off. "What are friends for?"

"Is that all we are? Just friends?" she asked, not sounding particularly concerned.

So, he didn't go into masculine panic mode. "In my world there isn't anything *just* about being a true friend."

"I understand that. All of my so-called friends dumped me when I walked out on Art. I didn't realize they were only interested in spending time with me if I came as part of a power couple."

"Even though he cheated on you?" Zephyr asked in disgust.

"Art wasn't the only one who believed that hoary old refrain he was so good at spouting."

"Which one is that?"

"All men cheat," she clarified.

"We don't."

"The jury is still out on that one, but I was not about to stay married to a man who believed infidelity was as inevitable as the tide."

"You know I think you made the right choice divorcing that louse." At least her family had finally come around to that conclusion as well, even if her former friends had not.

"Me, too. But unfortunately, *that louse* runs one of the most successful design houses in New York."

"Hence your move to Seattle."

"Exactly. There just wasn't room enough in The Big Apple for both his ego and my career." She smiled sadly.

The bastard she'd been married to had done his best to blackball her in the design community. Zephyr had returned the favor over the past two years and Très Bon no longer held its prestigious top position status. Arthur Bellingham's word might send ripples out in the city, but Zephyr Nikos sent out waves big enough to drown in the international community.

The bastard who had done his best to ruin Piper's life was on the slippery slope of business decline already. Art would only find himself in deep, murky waters when he got to the bottom, too.

Zephyr had never told Piper, of course. She hadn't been exposed to his ruthless streak and he saw no reason to change that.

"Well, I am glad you came to Seattle," he said.

"Again, me, too." She tugged off her jacket, revealing the silky singlet she wore beneath it, and the fact she *wasn't* wearing a bra. "I certainly made a better circle of friends."

"Oh, I am round now?" he asked, practically choking on his lust as her hardened nipples created shoals in the slinky fabric of her top.

He forcibly snapped his attention back to Athens's typically snarled traffic, lest he cause an accident or do a poor job avoiding one. He could hardly do what he was fantasizing to her body from a hospital bed.

Having her in peril of the same didn't even bear thinking of.

"Don't be smart." She tapped his leg, having the opposite effect to the one he was sure she meant it to. "I have other friends."

"Name one."

"Brandi."

"She is your assistant."

"I have friends," Piper insisted stubbornly. "There's a reason I'm not available every night to keep you entertained."

Which wasn't something he actually liked, so he let the subject drop.

Usually, Piper noticed every tiny detail of her surroundings, always looking for ways to improve her own sense of design and aesthetics. However, she barely noticed the earth tones and ultramodern, simplistic design features of the luxury spa Zephyr had chosen for their stay as he led her through the oversized lobby to the bank of elevators on the far side.

She was too busy soaking in his every feature, her senses starved for the sight, taste and feel of him.

The past month and a half had been harder than any separation they'd had to date. For her anyway. Maybe for Zephyr, too, if the number of calls and texts she'd gotten from him was anything to go on. They'd had prolonged times apart before, but not since they started having sex regularly six months ago. Still, it wasn't as if they were a couple. They were friends, who were also casual sex partners. At least that's what she'd been telling herself since the first time they'd passed that intimate boundary nine months ago.

That first time, she'd thought it would be a one-off, something to get the sexual tension that had been growing between them out of the way of their friendship. She'd been wrong.

They hadn't gotten physical again until three months later, but connected sexually several times a week since then. When he made it clear, again, that he did not see the sex as anything more than physical compatibility for stress release, she'd told herself she wasn't ready for a committed relationship, either, so that was just fine with her. Art had done a real number on her ability to trust and she had a business to build. She didn't have a place in her life for a full-time relationship.

The only problem was: she wasn't sure she believed her own rhetoric any longer. Her natural optimism was doing its best to overcome her painfully learnt lesson on the ways of men. *The fact she was having such a complicated internal monologue on the matter was telling in itself,* she thought with an internal sigh.

She'd been careful not to ask for promises Zephyr might break, or make commitments she wasn't ready for.

But she'd come to realize over the past six weeks—while subsisting on phone calls, texts, instant messaging and e-mail—that emotions didn't abide by agreements, verbal or otherwise. That refusing to make a vow didn't stop her heart from craving the security that promise implied. Nor did it stop her from living like she'd made her own promises.

She'd missed Zephyr more than she'd thought possible and wanted nothing more right now than to wrap herself up in him and soak in his essence.

He seemed to want the same thing. He hadn't stopped touching her since they left the airport. He'd laid his hand over hers between gear changes in the car and he'd kept his arm around her waist all the way to the room.

He opened the door with a flourish. "Here we are."

The suite reflected the minimalist décor from downstairs, but its spaciousness spoke of the ultimate in luxury. "This place is bigger than my apartment."

"My closet is bigger than your flat," he said, sounding unimpressed.

She grimaced at the truth of his words, but the curve of

her lips morphed into a smile from the heat burning in his brown eyes.

From the feel of his arousal when he'd first hugged and kissed her hello, and the sexual need intensifying his features then and now, she expected to be taken against the door with a minimum of foreplay.

But that didn't happen. He set her cases aside and then lifted her right into his arms, high against his chest, in a move that made her feel cherished rather than just wanted.

She quickly banished that thought even as her gasp of surprise escaped her. "Going he-man on me?"

"Spoiling you more like."

"Oh, really? I could get used to this," she teased.

He didn't bother with a reply, but didn't look too fazed at the prospect. So not good for the odd blips of emotion that had been pestering her lately. But that was one thing she could say about Zephyr Nikos, whether it be in his role as friend, boss or bed partner, the man did not stint on his generosity.

Despite his obvious desire, rather than showing mass amounts of impatience, he laid her gently on the big bed and seemed determined to reacquaint himself with every facet of her body. He drove her crazy with reticence while pumping her for information on her time away from him.

After he asked yet another question about her experience in the Midwest decorating the interior for a new office building, she laughed. "We spoke every day, Zephyr. I can't think of anything I didn't already tell you."

The gorgeous tycoon actually looked like he might be blushing, his dark eyes reflecting chagrin. "I was just curious."

"You know what I do on a job. I've done it for Stamos and Nikos Enterprises often enough."

"Did you like the Midwest better than Seattle?" he asked with what she thought was entirely mistimed curiosity.

"Are you kidding?"

His expression said clearly he wasn't.

"I love Seattle. The energy in the city is amazing." And he was there.

"That's good to know."

Suddenly, all his questions started to make sense. "You heard."

CHAPTER TWO

ZEPHYR tried to look innocent.

"How? Who told you?"

"Does it matter? Information is more lucrative than platinum in my business."

"Did you seriously think Pearson Property Developments could offer me a better situation than your company already has done?"

"Money isn't your only consideration, it isn't even your main one, or you would have accepted my job offer by now."

It was true. She would make a lot more money working for him as an employee whose overheads were absorbed by the company rather than as a fledgling design business that sucked up the vast majority of the not-insubstantial fees charged to her clients.

"So, you thought I might like the Midwest enough to take Pearson's job offer?" She couldn't imagine it and disbelief colored her voice.

"They didn't just offer you a job."

"No, they also offered a contract for several projects they have in the pipeline over the next two years." While still leaving her an independent operator, the offer would provide the kind of security most up-and-coming designers dreamed about.

If living in a landlocked state without a single authentic

Vietnamese or Thai restaurant was what she wanted. It wasn't. She was too fond of the diversified and active culture of Seattle.

"I've gotten too spoiled to big-city living. The only Thai restaurant I found was run by a man named Arnie who thinks a good curry comes with corn-on-the-cob."

Zephyr shuddered. "So, you are not taking the contract."

"Doing so would have made it impossible to do this property. I wasn't willing to give up a chance at decorating a specialty resort in paradise for re-creating my first design in a series of cookie-cutter office buildings."

One of the things she and Art had disagreed on, besides the whole issue of marital fidelity, was her need to create, not merely re-create. For Art, the bottom line was always money. While Piper craved security, she needed the chance to stretch her artistic muscles just as much.

"I'm glad."

She smiled. "Good."

"I'm equally pleased you are here with me now." For a man like Zephyr, that was quite an admission.

It deserved rewarding, at the very least reciprocating honesty. Emotion she was doing her best to suppress colored her single-word answer. "Ditto."

He made a sexy sound, very much like a growl, before pulling her to him for a scorching kiss. Finally.

She'd missed him; she'd missed this so much. Being touched. Being held. She'd gotten very spoiled to seeing him so frequently.

She threw herself into the kiss without the least resistance. She adored his lovemaking, but she could do this for hours.

And from the way his lips moved against hers, so could he.

She felt herself being lifted and then she was straddling his thighs, her skirt rucked up around her hips. The mattress was firm enough to support his sitting up easily. What brand was it? She couldn't help wondering.

And then all work-related thoughts disappeared as her

brain focused on the only thing that mattered right now, the sensation of being held and kissed by the most amazing man she'd ever met.

His mouth fit over hers perfectly. And he tasted like her idea of heaven. He deepened the kiss, but with no sense of urgency, telling her silently that they had all the time in the world. He was the only man she'd ever known who treated kissing like an end unto itself.

The kiss broke for a moment, their lips sliding apart in a natural movement. He caressed her cheek and temple with his lips.

She smiled, warmed clear through and pleased by the fact he hadn't just missed sex with her. He seemed to have missed their connection almost as much as she had.

"I'm surprised you're not tearing my clothes off after six weeks going without," she whispered, the hushed quiet around them feeling almost sacred.

Then a chilling thought took her. Maybe he hadn't gone without. Maybe that's why he was so relaxed. They'd never made the commitment toward monogamy. He could very well have found someone else back in Seattle.

"I kept myself busy at work. With Neo cutting back his hours to spend more time with Cass, there's a lot of reorganization of responsibilities going on." He gave her gentle baby kisses all over face and neck between words. "Even if you had been in Seattle, I would barely have seen you over the past six weeks."

Which implied he hadn't been with anyone else, either.

"I didn't realize it was that bad." He'd mentioned something to that effect, but she'd thought he was just trying to make her feel better.

She should have known better. For all his apparent affability, Zephyr Nikos was an almost brutally honest man. He'd warned her early in their association that he didn't do "sensitive" and he hoped she could handle candor, even when it meant criticism. He'd been referring to their work association, but she'd gotten the impression he was that way on a personal level as well.

Then, after they'd become friends, she'd gotten proof of her impression. So, why did she keep looking for evidence to the contrary now that they were involved more intimately? On a physical level anyway.

He pulled his head back and met her eyes with a sardonic expression. "Neo is a force of nature. We've had to restructure our head office entirely, promoting several people into positions of greater authority while hiring others and training them to take over the new vacancies."

"With you picking up the slack."

The signs of exhaustion were there and she couldn't believe it had taken her this long to notice. Her delight in being in his company again was her only excuse. Dark shadows under Zephyr's eyes, his vitality muted—she wasn't the only one who needed a couple of days without work.

"It is worth it to see him so happy." There was something in Zephyr's tone. Not quite envy, not exactly sadness, but definite sincerity.

It confused her.

"I can't imagine Neo in love," was all she said, though.

"You've only met him a few times."

"And he's always the same. Intense. Focused. Almost dour." There was no almost about it, but she didn't want to offend Zephyr by calling his best friend and business partner an emotionless robot.

"Cass makes him laugh." The strange tone was there again and no more comprehensible to Piper.

Regardless, she could not picture Neo Stamos laughing. "He really *must* be in love."

"Yes."

She might not be able to interpret that tone, but Piper did know something about it bothered her. She scooted up his lap so the silk panties covering her were directly over the hard bulge behind his zipper.

Whatever was going on in Zephyr's head, his desire for her had not abated by even a centimeter.

He needed to relax and forget about Stamos & Nikos Enterprises for a while. She knew just how to help him do that.

She leaned forward and spoke against his lips. "No more talking, Zephyr."

"You have something better to do with my lips?" Every word brushed his lips provocatively against hers.

"Absolutely." She drew out the syllables, making each one a minicaress leading up to when she pressed their mouths together with serious intent.

He let her control the kiss for several tantalizing minutes she knew would not last. Allowing her tongue to tease his, he kept his hands locked onto her hips while she tunneled her fingers through his gorgeous dark hair. She rocked against him, bringing them both moan-producing pleasure.

One of the things she most adored about making love with this man was how totally into it he got. And how much he liked when she did the same. He never made her feel like a freak for enjoying sex. Art had often made cutting comments about her behavior in bed, reining in her abandon. And then he'd had the temerity to say that all men cheated because they couldn't get what they needed from one woman. But especially their wives.

Bull. Art hadn't been willing to take what Piper had been prepared to give. Zephyr, on the other hand, never made her feel dirty for getting lost in the physical. Her passion did not intimidate or disgust him. Not on any level.

Because his passion was just as deep and consuming. He didn't posture or pretend. He wasn't a man driven by appearances, like her ex-husband.

Zephyr did not worry about wrinkling or staining his clothes when their desires got in the way of a neat and tidy disrobing. Like now. It was clear from the way he touched and responded to her that he wasn't thinking about anything but the pleasure between them, the way their bodies pressed and writhed together in primal need.

It wasn't in the predatory nature of her tycoon to remain passive for long. And she waited with adrenaline-fueled anticipation for him to make his move.

He did not disappoint her, erupting from his sitting position to spin them around and lay her against the bed once more. He came down over her, his body heat and the strength of his bulging muscles surrounding her with his solid presence. A frisson of atavistic pleasure rolled straight down her spine directly to her feminine core.

She would never tell him, but she loved when her *über*-sophisticated lover went caveman on her. His big body rubbed against hers; his hands were everywhere. But then so were hers. He touched her through her clothes, then shoved her silk top up her torso with a growling wound deep in his chest. Masculine fingers caressed her stomach, circling her belly button before moving up to gently mold her unfettered breasts and pluck at her nipples.

Urgent sounds of need slipped from her mouth to his. Her body rocked upward of its own volition, sharp talons of sexual hunger piercing her and making her muscles tense and strain.

If he didn't claim her body with his soon, she was going to lose her mind. Or take over. Somehow.

One of his hands slid between them, then the pad of his thumb was exactly where she needed it to be, caressing her swollen clitoris right through the silk of her panties.

The pleasure built at light speed and she felt her climax taking her over before she'd even gotten a chance to start really aching for it. Of course, she'd been hungry for his brand of loving since the last night they spent together six weeks ago.

His voracious kiss swallowed her scream of undeniable

pleasure. It went on and on and on and on in an unending cascade of bliss that drained all coherent thought from her mind.

Then the caressing finger moved away and she floated on a haze of satiation. It was temporary, because she knew he wasn't finished, or even close to it.

The sound of a condom wrapper tearing filtered through her consciousness, but her eyes wouldn't focus. Everything was blurred by the mind-numbing pleasure she had just experienced.

It was her fragile panties tearing away from her body that got her attention, though. The look of near animalistic carnality hardening his features made her insides clench in wanton hunger. He pressed against her slick opening with his latex-covered shaft.

And then he was inside her, his long and thick erection filling her like no other man could.

He looked down at her, his dark eyes practically black with desire. "Okay?"

She answered with a tilt of her pelvis, taking him in as deep as he would go. The feel of his blunt head pushing inexorably against her cervix sparked another orgasm, this one deep inside, an intense contraction of her womb that tilted between pain and pleasure.

Though she didn't think she'd done anything to reveal the shock of internal delight, his openly feral gaze gleamed with satisfaction.

And then he started moving, setting a rhythm that both demanded her participation and coaxed it from her with jolt after jolt of electric pleasure.

They moved together with an urgency that would not be denied. It was only minutes before he was tearing his lips from her and roaring out his release.

Shockingly, her body contracted around him in a third muted climax sparked by the final swelling of his hardness pressing against her G-spot with inflexible pressure.

He said a four-letter word.

"I prefer the term *making love*." She grinned tiredly, her entire body boneless from the overwhelming cataclysm that had been their joining.

He barked out a laugh and shook his head. "That was incredible."

"That's one word for it." She looked down their bodies. They were both practically dressed. Clothes unzipped and moved out of the way only as much as absolutely necessary to make their copulating possible. "Earthshaking is another."

"That's two words."

"And two more words for you—still dressed."

His gaze traveled the path hers had and he took in their still dressed condition with widening eyes. "Unbelievable."

He sounded as shocked as she felt, which struck her as unbelievably funny and she started laughing. Soon his laughter joined hers and he had to grab the condom before rolling off her as their humor continued unabated for long minutes.

He stood up and disposed of the condom before yanking off slacks that looked like they belonged on the jumble heap. "I wonder what the dry cleaner is going to think of that."

"Do you really care?"

"No." He finished undressing and then started working on her clothes. "Your panties are goners, but I think the dry cleaner can save your skirt."

"You could have the decency to sound at least a little apologetic about that."

"Why? What is a single pair of panties in comparison to the pleasure we both just enjoyed?"

Too true, but it wouldn't do for her to say so. "They were my favorite pair."

"Oh, really?" He gave her his patented doubtful frown that had sent more than one negotiator toppling toward defeat. "I don't recall seeing them before. Ever. And I think I have more than a nodding acquaintance with the delectable bits of fabric you choose to cover your own even more enticing bits."

"Charmer." Then she gave him a fake pout. "I bought them new for today."

"So how could they be your favorites?"

"They were my *new* favorites."

"Well, they're rubbish now." And really? He didn't sound even sort of bothered by that.

Which she liked. A lot. Still, she wasn't ready to cede the game completely. "I thought you'd like them."

"I did. Couldn't you tell?"

She laughed, feeling joyous and free. "I'm only going to forgive you because I had multiple orgasms."

"Three of them. In a very short period," he added with well-deserved smugness. "It makes me wonder what I can do with the rest of the night."

What he did was make love to her until she passed out from exhaustion sometime around dawn…after no less than three more orgasms.

They slept in, waking at the tail end of the morning to share a decadent brunch. Then he took her to the Acropolis. She'd watched a travel video about the temple ruins found there, but nothing prepared her for how it felt actually standing where many claimed the modern constructs of Western Civilization had been born. Maybe not everyone reacted like she did, but she felt a sense of profundity that she could not shake.

She could not help staring at the Parthenon in absolute awe.

When she told Zephyr about it, he did not laugh at her like Art would have done.

Zephyr only nodded, his expression serious. "This is not just a pile of ingeniously put-together stone. We are standing on history. You cannot dismiss something like that."

"That's why your developments are so special, isn't it?"

"Because I recognize history when I see it?" he asked with underlying amusement.

She reached out and took his hand. She could not help

herself. She needed to touch this incredible man. "Because you recognize the unique flavor of wherever you are and rather than try to change it, you seek to enhance it."

Very few developers could make that claim, and none as successful as Stamos & Nikos Enterprises.

"Neo and I learned early to see the good in wherever we were." He laced their fingers together, giving her a look that implied he wasn't just talking about property development.

"Even the orphanage?" she asked softly.

"I admit I saw more good there than Neo did."

"I'm not surprised."

He shrugged.

"That's a pretty nice talent to have. I wish I'd had it as a child like you did." She might have found moving around as much as her family had done easier than she had. "Heck, I wouldn't mind having it now."

"Don't play down your strengths. That was one of the first characteristics I admired in you."

"Seriously?"

"Definitely. When you look at a property, you do not see what is, but what could be."

"That's not the same thing."

"No, but it comes from the same attitude."

"Then why was I such a miserable kid?" She felt like an idiot asking that. She'd been a grown-up for a long time. The little girl that found changing homes and schools every couple of years so traumatizing was long gone.

"It wasn't an inability to find the good in each new situation that your father's military career led you to that made you so unhappy. It was the fact you found so much to love and enjoy in each new place and that got ripped from you with every new reassignment."

Feeling light-headed, and not from the panoramic view of Athens, she swallowed after developeing a suddenly dry throat. Because Zephyr was exactly right. Every time she had found the place she wanted to occupy in her new world, she had been ripped away from it.

But still. "Lots of kids grow up the way I did."

"That doesn't make it any easier on each one that does it. There were more than two dozen other children in the orphanage my mother abandoned me to. That reality did not make my own situation any easier to accept when she left me behind."

"Your mother *abandoned you* to the orphanage?"

Zephyr walked to a viewpoint that overlooked Hadrian's Arch. He still had hold of Piper's hand, so she came with him. Feeling like the only connection he had with the present was their entwined fingers, he could not believe he had shared that information with Piper. He'd never even talked about it to Neo. Yet, he knew he was going to tell Piper the truth now.

Maybe not all, but at least some. He just didn't understand why.

"How old were you?" she asked, after several moments of somber quiet between them.

"Four, almost five." He looked down at her to gauge his tenderhearted lover's reaction.

She did not disappoint him. Her pretty blue eyes glazed over in shock. "I thought you were a baby, or something."

"No. My mother was a prostitute." Again, a sense of utter unreality that he should be telling Piper these things assailed him. "One of her clients fell in love with her and wanted to marry her, but he didn't want a living reminder of the life she'd led before they met."

As an adult man, he could almost understand that. Not forgive, but understand. As a child who had adored his mother, the only bright constant in his short life, the one he had relied on entirely for acceptance and love, he hadn't been so wise. Neither his child's mind, nor the heart he'd later encased in impenetrable stone, had been able to comprehend his mother's actions, or even her husband's attitude.

The man had been kind enough to the small boy the few

times they met before he decided to buy Leda's freedom from her *procurer*, Zephyr's father.

"But you were *her child*!" Piper's obvious shock nearly ripped her hand from his grasp.

He tightened his grip, unwilling to let her go. "My mother visited. Once a month, but I learned to wish she wouldn't."

"Because she never took you with her when she left."

"No." No matter how he'd begged at first.

"When was the last time you spoke to her?"

"Last month." But he hadn't seen her since he'd run away from the orphanage with Neo, this time by *Zephyr's* choice.

Piper stared up at him, her eyes swimming with emotion, her mouth opening and closing, but no sound coming out.

He took pity on her clear inability to fathom this state of affairs. "I contacted her after I made my first million. She was glad to hear from me."

"You sound like that surprised you."

"It did. Even though I was now wealthy, there was no guarantee she would want the reminder of her past."

"You thought money was all you had to give her."

Naturally. He'd never met a woman who didn't appreciate financial gifts, his mother setting that precedent early for his young mind. "Why would I believe anything else?"

"She was glad you were safe, though, wasn't she? I bet she cried that first time you called her."

That time and almost every one since. "You are right." Not that he understood why.

If his disappearance was such a hardship on his mother, surely she would not have dumped him at the orphanage in the first place? Nevertheless, she had not abandoned him entirely.

"She paid the orphanage to care for me." He had discovered that when he made his first donation to the home long before he amassed his first million.

It was the reason he had contacted her later. Without the knowledge she had attempted to provide for him in some way, he did not think he ever would have. But nothing could have altered the path he had taken with his father.

"Are we going to see her while we are here?" Piper's voice dripped with the emotion clouding her expression.

"No."

"Of course, I'm sorry." From looking on the verge of tears, Piper went to embarrassment in a single breath. "There's no reason to take your friend to visit your mother."

"It's not that. She would like you." How could she not? Piper was a very likable woman. "However, I have no intention of seeing my mother."

"What? Why not? Surely we have time. Even if she lives on one of the islands. We can skip the sightseeing."

"She lives in Athens. I bought her a house in Kifissia." The distance between that district and the one he had been born in was measured in more than kilometers, though.

Piper's brow furrowed. "According to the guidebook in our suite, that's the elite part of town."

"Is that what it said?"

"Well, as good as."

"The book is right. The wealthy have inhabited Kifissia for generations."

"And you bought your mother a house there."

He shrugged. What did Piper want him to say? He had wanted to give his mother a physical break from the past.

"Yet you are not going to visit her."

"No," he confirmed.

"But…"

"I have not seen her in more than twenty years, Piper."

"But you said you spoke last month." The confusion on Piper's face was adorable.

He kissed her. Not passionately, but he could not resist the innocent incomprehension covering her features.

"It was her birthday. So, I spoke to her."

"You call her once a year, on her birthday?" Piper guessed.

"Yes." The year after he first reconnected with Leda, he had made the mistake of asking what she would like for her birthday.

He'd become too ingrained in American customs. And he'd wanted the excuse to give her something nice, something to show her and the man she had married that Zephyr wasn't such a dead loss after all. He wasn't a lame puppy to be abandoned.

But his mother hadn't asked for a designer handbag, or a new television. She'd only wanted one thing. For Zephyr to call her once a year on her birthday, so she could know he was doing all right. She could follow his success in the papers now, but he still made that call.

Once a year.

"Does she call you?"

"I have asked her not to, unless there is a problem with my brother or sister." Keeping his mother at a distance was necessary and he could not change that.

"You have a brother and sister?"

He had expected some kind of criticism for his coldness toward his mother, but Piper hadn't focused on a situation he could not change. She'd zeroed in on the one reality *he* found truly important. His sister and brother.

"They are half siblings, but I feel a responsibility toward them nonetheless."

"How old are they?"

"Iola is twenty-nine. She is married to a good man and has three children of her own."

Six years younger than him, his sister had been born a year and a half after he went into the home.

His mother had missed her visit with him that month and the one after. He'd thought she'd finally grown tired of coming to see him and wasn't coming back. But she'd returned and she'd had a beautiful baby with her when she did.

"Have you met the children?"

"Yes, Iola insisted."

"You sound like you don't understand why."

"I'm the bastard child her mother gave birth to when living a life they would all rather forget happened. My sister doesn't even remember meeting me. She was too young the last time I saw her."

"Your mother brought her to visit?"

"Yes."

"That was cruel."

He shrugged. To his way of thinking, it had been much more cruel when his mother stopped bringing Iola. Some might have thought he would be jealous of the baby, but Zephyr had adored Iola from the very beginning. He had been heartbroken when his mother's husband had insisted Leda stop bringing his sister to visit when she was two.

But just like when he had begged to be taken with her, his mother turned deaf ears to his pleas to see the little girl he had allowed himself to love.

"I thought she was the most amazing being ever. I was in awe of her."

"What did she think of you?"

"I don't know. Her father did not want her to wonder about me, so my mother stopped bringing her on the visits when she was old enough to begin remembering them. My mother only brought my brother a handful of times as an infant for the same reason."

"Clearly, they *don't* want to forget you. Not if your sister insisted you meet her children."

"I take care of them." And even his stony heart could be moved by the little ones who called him Uncle Zee.

"You think that's the only reason they want you in their lives?"

"Why else?"

"Maybe for the same reason I'd want you in my life even if I didn't work with you." How could he be so unaware of his own true worth? she wondered.

"Would you?"

"Yes."

He didn't believe her, but he appreciated the sentiment.

"Does your brother-in-law work for you?" Piper asked.

"How did you know?"

"You said you take care of them. Does your brother work for you as well?"

"No. He's academically brilliant. He's finishing his doctoral thesis in physics right now."

"Let me guess, you've paid for his education."

"Naturally."

She threw her arms around him and kissed him, far more exuberantly than he had kissed her just a moment ago. "You are an amazing man, Zephyr Nikos."

He shook his head, but he was no idiot. He kissed her back and enjoyed the moment while it lasted, all the while wondering what in the hell was wrong with him that he had shared so much with Piper.

Maybe this friends-who-shared-sexual-intimacy wasn't such a good idea after all. He couldn't give her love and this openness was bound to give her the wrong impression.

CHAPTER THREE

HE TOOK her to the Plaka after she'd soaked in all the history she could from the Acropolis ruins. That, and the fact that visiting hours were over. He could have arranged for special dispensation but wanted to take her shopping in the ancient marketplace.

It was a tourist's paradise and Piper in tourist mode was completely charming. It also put them back on the kind of solid ground he understood. They found a shop that made authentic reproductions of ancient Greek jewelry and he bought her a necklace that would not have looked out of place on the neck of a senator's wife.

Piper had balked at the cost, but he had stood firm. If he wanted to buy her a souvenir of their time in Athens, he would.

He could afford to spoil her and she deserved to be spoiled. Especially after the way that bastard of an ex-husband had treated her. Zephyr would not pretend to give her love as Art had, but he could afford to give her gifts. And he would.

Later that night, on the terrace of an exclusive restaurant, Piper found herself enjoying the understated, elegant décor that managed to still convey the flavor of Athens. Like most Greek restaurants, the majority of the seating was outside. However, this restaurant did not have the crowded, noisy ambiance of the cafés in the Plaka.

As much as she had enjoyed the historic shopping district

closed off to automobile traffic, she appreciated the relative quiet of their current setting. Very much.

"Is this a favorite haunt of yours when you are in the country?"

"It is actually." Zephyr's brows furrowed. "How did you know?"

"I don't imagine the staff know most American businessmen by name, no matter how rich and powerful."

Looking oh so sexy in a light Armani sweater and body-hugging designer jeans, his lips quirked in his signature wry smile. "Point."

She was glad to see his smile. He'd seemed to draw back emotionally after opening up to her on the Acropolis. It was as if he regretted sharing so much about his past and needed to bring their focus firmly back to the present.

She could understand that. Zephyr was not a guy to wallow in emotion. Heck, he wasn't a guy to feel emotion a lot of the time, as far as she could see. But she'd realized something as they shopped in the Plaka—she felt plenty toward Zephyr. In fact, she was drowning in emotion for him and that emotion only had one name. Love.

"Thank you for sharing this place with me." She brushed her fingers over the gorgeous necklace he'd bought her earlier that day. "Thank you for everything."

The stones were warm from her body, but her heart was even warmer. He had insisted a kiss would make the purchase fully worthwhile. Since her kisses were free, she'd thought nothing of giving him one. Right there, in front of the proprietor, who had grinned and said something in Greek that made Zephyr chuckle.

Piper wasn't just feeling spoiled, she was feeling cherished and that was dangerous, she knew.

"It is my pleasure."

"You say that a lot." She smiled up at him.

"And it is true. You are an easy companion, Piper."

"I'm glad you think so. I don't hate your company, either."

"That is a relief. I would not like to think you'd been giving me pity sex all this time."

She couldn't help laughing at that bit of ridiculousness. "Right. Pity sex. I don't see it." Or feel it. No woman would pity this man. Desire him? Yes. Crave his kisses? Definitely. Hunger for his touch? Without doubt.

But pity? Nope. No way.

"I'm relieved to hear it."

She felt heat climb her cheeks and she shook her head. "Stop teasing me and eat your appetizer."

Surprisingly, her tycoon listened and did exactly that.

They were halfway through the appetizer when she asked something she'd been curious about for a while. "Are you going to be Neo's best man in the wedding?"

"Naturally."

"Are you looking forward to it?" she teased, sure he would grimace and give a negative.

But he smiled instead and said quite decisively, "Yes."

"You are?" She had not expected that.

"Of course. I worried that Neo had forgotten his dreams of home and family under the pressure of building our empire. When we first left Greece, that was all he'd talk about, how he was going to make something of himself and then make a proper family. He stopped talking about it maybe two years after we settled in Seattle."

"But you didn't want him to forget it entirely?" Wow, that was not an ambition she could picture Zephyr encouraging.

"No. He deserves a family, a home that is more than a place to live."

"Those are some pretty traditional sentiments for a self-admitted playboy."

"What can I say? I am a traditional guy."

That made her laugh. "I don't think so."

"What? Just because I am not married does not mean I never desire to enter the state." He didn't look like he was kidding.

But she couldn't get past the feeling he had to be pulling her leg. Zephyr was the original no-commitment guy. He'd made that clear from the very beginning of their sexual relationship. So much so, that she had assumed the first time had been a one-off.

He'd shocked her by coming back for more when they worked together on the next project, and continuing to see her in Seattle after that. But he'd been smart to give her the time to accept the change in their relationship, so she was ready to accept the new "friends with benefits" nature of it.

"You look flummoxed."

"I feel a little flummoxed," she admitted.

"I do not know why. It is the American dream, not just the Greek one, is it not? One day, I will find the right woman." He gave a self-deprecating smile that gave her butterflies. "Hell, I may even fall in love as Neo has done."

Those words felt like an arrow to her heart, because they implied he had not found that woman, therefore that woman could not be her. After finally coming to terms with her own feelings, that was a double blow to her heart. Her hand went to her necklace again, this time gaining no sense of comfort from the feel of the precious metal and stones. You had to love someone to cherish them.

So, what did that make this gift and all the other gifts he'd given her?

Unfortunately, after hearing his story earlier she feared she knew. This was Zephyr's relationship currency. Gifts and money. Not love. Not for the mother who had hurt him and not for Piper, either.

"You don't seem like the home-and-hearth type, Zephyr," she couldn't resist saying. "You live in the ultimate bachelor pad and you've dated far and wide. And deep and long besides."

Besides which he saw his relationships with his mother and siblings as monetary transactions.

"As was Neo before he met Cass. Me? I am as desirous of making my mark on the world in that way as any other man."

"You're serious?" The words were just a formality, though. There could be no doubt from his tone or his expression.

He was dead serious.

"Why wouldn't I be? Regardless of what I just said, I do not anticipate falling in love like Neo, but one day I *will* marry and procreate. Why build an empire if I have no intention of leaving it to someone?"

She didn't mention his nieces and nephew. Clearly, that wasn't what he meant. Zephyr wanted his *own* family. "But you don't think you will ever fall in love?"

"No."

That made more sense, even if it hurt enough to make it difficult to breathe.

"But…"

"But what? You loved your ex-husband, yes?"

She grimaced. "Yes."

"And did that bring you happiness?"

"No, but that doesn't mean I don't think love can happen, or make me happy when it does."

"Perhaps it will happen for you again one day."

"Maybe it will." It already had—with him—and his revelations on the Acropolis had only cemented that fact.

However, she could see it wasn't a truth he would be pleased if she shared. No matter how much that situation hurt her, she could not change it. She suddenly realized she was very likely to pay the price for another woman's actions. Actions that were decades old, but had not lost the power to hurt or mold Zephyr's actions.

But Zephyr's heart was not available to her and might never be.

His lips twisted in distaste. "Love is a messy emotion."

"No question, but it's good, too." Surely he could see that, especially now that Neo was so happily in that state?

"You don't regret loving Art?" Zephyr asked with calculated cool.

"No. I regret that he was a cheater and a liar and that his love was more words than substance."

"How is that different from regretting loving him?"

"My love was a good thing."

"That ended up causing you pain," he observed wryly.

She couldn't deny it. Loving Art had nearly destroyed her on every level. And loving Zephyr didn't look like it was going to be a much better prospect. At least she knew where she stood with him, though.

That was something, wasn't it?

Zephyr gave one of those self-deprecating smiles he used when negotiating and it made her stomach clench to have him use it on her. "Look, I'm not trying to be the Scrooge of happily ever after, but you and I both know someone loving you is no guarantee they won't betray you."

"That doesn't mean you shouldn't open yourself to love at all." She tried to keep the desperation his attitude evoked out of her voice. It wasn't his fault she'd been dumb enough to fall in love with the wrong man. Again.

"It works for me."

And she couldn't fault him for his attitude. Now that she knew his mother had abandoned him to build a better life for herself, Piper couldn't help understanding Zephyr's distrust of love.

"But Neo loves Cassandra and vice-versa. Or so you said."

"Cassandra is one woman in a million."

The pain those words caused took Piper by surprise, making her heart cramp and her whole chest cavity hurt. Because they implied she was *not* such a woman. Who was she kidding? Certainly not herself. This whole conversation put Zephyr's attitude toward her in stark relief.

He didn't love her. Not even a little. He didn't anticipate loving her, either. Not ever. Which was really not what she wanted to hear. The pain coursing through her mocked all the promises she'd made to herself after walking away from Art. She wouldn't lose her livelihood when she and Zephyr's sexual relationship ended, but she wasn't sure her heart would survive, even if her business did.

Piper was head over heels in love with a man who did not believe in the concept for himself, and moreover he looked forward to marrying one day. Only Zephyr clearly did not intend that woman to be her. Not when he so blithely told her maybe *she* would find love again one day.

He'd reneged on his own words of maybe finding love and she felt like retracting hers as well. Was the prospect of love worth the possibility of this pain again?

She remembered the last time she had felt this awful inability to breathe. It had been when she realized once and for all that Art did not love her and never had. And once again, for her pride's sake and maybe even for Zephyr's sake, she had to hide the devastation going on inside her.

"I think you might be right," she said, trying not to choke on the words.

"About what?"

"I do a pretty sucky job deciding who to fall in love with."

"I couldn't agree more."

She laughed, but felt no humor. "Thanks."

"I've no interest in talking about Art Bellingham anymore."

"Trust me, this whole conversation is leaving me cold."

His eyes narrowed, but he smiled. One of his "armor smiles" again and she wanted to be sick. "So, tell me what you want to do tomorrow."

She needed to do a better job of hiding her emotions. Starting now. "I'm a museum freak. I'd really like to see the National Archaeological Museum, the Acropolis Museum and maybe the Benaki Museum."

"That's quite a list considering you did not plan to sightsee on this trip."

"I spent the time you were in the shower pouring over the guidebook in our hotel suite."

"Ah. So, tomorrow is to be a gluttony of museums."

"If you'd rather do something else, I can find my own way to the museums."

His brow quirked at this suggestion. "There is nothing I would rather do than spend the time with you. I grew up in this city. I have seen it all."

She couldn't see him visiting the Acropolis when he was living on the streets, but she didn't say anything. It was taking all her wherewithal to tamp down emotions she had not fully acknowledged before today, feelings that would be unwelcome to their intended recipient and would cause her nothing but aching heartbreak.

"As long as we are planning our schedule, what would you like to do the day after tomorrow?"

"I thought we were flying out to the island."

"I've got a helicopter booked for late afternoon. I wanted to maximize your off time."

"You spoil me." And he did. He might not love her, but he was her friend and he cared enough to want her to be rested and happy. "This isn't supposed to be a vacation."

"Yes, in fact, these days are intended as exactly that. Surprise to you though they were."

"But the day after tomorrow was supposed to be work." She wasn't sure which would be worse, spending more time sightseeing or being stuck in close proximity with him on a private island paradise.

"So, I changed the schedule a little."

"Whatever you want."

He frowned. "I want you to enjoy yourself."

"I am in Greece, what is not to enjoy?"

"Then you will approve of a visit to Sounion and the temple ruins for Trident there?" he asked.

"Sure, that would be fine."

"Would you prefer to do something else?"

"No, not at all." It really didn't matter. She needed to come to terms with her own inner revelations and his as well. The setting for doing that hardly mattered.

"Then, Trident's Temple it is."

She nodded. "Thank you."

"Think nothing of it. I knew it had to bother you to be visiting Greece and only see a small barely developed island the whole time you were here. You've got far too curious and adventurous a nature to be content with that."

"You know me well." On the surface anyway.

He'd be shocked out of his Gucci leather loafers to discover she was in love with him. And not in a good way.

That night, their lovemaking was slow and intense. Zephyr unwrapped her like a fragile gift of immeasurable value, and she tried to take it at face value, unable to deal with the pain of dwelling on emotions she could not change. On either of their parts.

They did not join until he had reacquainted himself with every inch of her skin. But his behavior was so at odds with his implication at dinner—that she was not a special woman in his life—that as wonderful as it was, a curious sense of dissonance flavored their intimacy for Piper.

Afterward, silent tears of confused emotions tracked down her cheeks in the dark. She fell asleep wishing she'd remained blind to her feelings, and if not hers at least his.

Piper woke the next morning experiencing yet another set of contradictory feelings. As always, when she woke in Zephyr's arms, she felt safe, cared for, cherished even. Only this morning, that sense of rightness fought with her new knowledge. The absolute certainty that Zephyr did not love her, the possibility that he never would and the probability that he would eventually walk away. At least from their sexual intimacy.

She hadn't meant to fall in love, but she'd done it anyway. And looking back, she didn't see how she could have stopped herself. Zephyr was all that she could desire in both a friend and a lover.

They shared many of the same interests. That's how their friendship had started. She'd discovered he shared her love of European football. They watched the matches, rooting for opposite teams and yelling at the field officials in equal measure. Later, she'd learned he also found museums and art galleries as fascinating as she did, as well as being passionately interested in world politics just as she was.

He was more than a good friend, he was the best. He didn't just enjoy the same interests she did, he cared about her and watched over her. He'd helped her build her business by recommending her to other developers, he'd even taken care of her once when she had the flu. He'd done his utmost to provide her a miniholiday and make it special. And he'd succeeded.

He treated her like a queen, never dismissing her intelligence or condescending to her. She snuggled into his strong arms, sensual pleasure running up her spine as he brushed his leg across her thigh in his sleep. And he made love to her like the world's most accomplished gigolo. She could not forget that important little fact.

Imagining what Zephyr would think of being compared to a sexual mercenary, she had to smile. Rather than take offense, the arrogant tycoon would probably preen. His sexual prowess was a source of pride for him. If only he was as open to love as he was to making love, she would not be in such a quandary.

Unhappy with her thoughts and the conclusions she felt drawn to because of them, she lay beside him, watching his gorgeous face in repose.

A dark lock of his hair fell over his forehead, doing nothing to make him look less intimidating, even in sleep. She'd always heard even the most ruthless men looked younger and more vulnerable in their sleep, but not Zephyr. Although he was unconscious to the world, he still did not relax completely. He appeared ready to wake and jump into the crowded moments of his day at any moment.

Had he learned that type of subconscious awareness living with his mother in the seedy underworld of Athens, in the orphanage or on the streets, where he had fought for a chance at a worthwhile life? After their discussion at the Acropolis, aspects of his personality that had always intrigued her made more sense.

When she had first met Zephyr, she had believed he was a charming, rather laid-back businessman. Watching him in action at work, she had soon learned differently. While Zephyr appeared to be relaxed, even borderline indolent, he kept meticulous track of every aspect of his developments.

He had a knack for keeping even the most artistic temperament on track and on schedule. There was a certain element of ruthlessness she'd seen under the surface that never quite broke through his "let's cooperate and get this job done" businessman's façade. It only showed in a quick comment here, a directed instruction there, all delivered with that game-face smile she'd hated having directed at her during dinner the night before.

But when Zephyr Nikos spoke, everyone listened. *Everyone*. He was brilliant. He was wealthy. He was a true force to be reckoned with. Honestly? She wasn't sure what he was doing with her, a woman struggling to build an interior design firm in Seattle after her ex-husband shredded her reputation in New York.

He might be fantastic for her, but she wasn't really in his league, which only made their friendship that much more precious and their pseudo-lovers relationship that much more difficult to understand from his point of view.

Falling in love with him might have been inevitable, but getting involved sexually had not. She'd had a choice and she'd made it believing she could handle the limitations of what he was offering. She'd been mistaken. Spectacularly so.

How could she have been so stupid? She really did pick badly when it came to choosing men to love.

First, there had been Art, who had seemed like the perfect source of stability, but who had in fact destroyed her security. Then, there was Zephyr, who seemed so charming and open on the surface, but who was actually more closed off than any man she had ever known.

He only lost control in one setting that she knew of—and she knew him as well as anyone, besides maybe Neo Stamos. Zephyr lost control when they made love.

He had from the very beginning, which was why she'd been so sure their intimacy would end up a one-off. He'd looked positively shell-shocked after that first time, his usually perfectly groomed hair askew, and his big body glistening with sweat. She'd been so turned on by his overall state of dishabille; she had initiated another round of lovemaking.

He'd acquiesced soon enough, but the next morning, she'd woken alone and they hadn't mentioned the sex in any shape or form the next time they spoke. They'd been at the tail end of another job together when the sexual tension thrumming between them blew up into another bout of no-holds-barred sex.

And Piper realized now, that was when she had started really falling for the billionaire tycoon. No matter what she'd told herself at the time about commitment-free sex with a friend. She'd been allowed to see a side of Zephyr Nikos that he showed to no one else. Doing so had captured and enthralled her.

Even more so when he had admitted what she had already suspected to be true after his reaction to their first time—that he was not the same with other women. Unfortunately, Piper had allowed herself to build emotional ties on that flimsy pretext, while ominously lying to herself about what was going on in her own heart the whole time.

But was the pretext so flimsy?

Despite what his words the night before had implied, she

was special to him. They were friends and he had few enough of those, no matter how he liked to tease Neo to the contrary. Piper and Zephyr's sexual relationship had already lasted longer than any other one he'd had as well. And she already knew it drew out a side in Zephyr he did not regularly let loose.

So, in all three of those instances, she was not business as usual for the tycoon. Add that to the fact he was vacationing for the first time since she'd known him, *with her and for her benefit*, and it all added up to something special. Right?

Or was she grasping at straws as she had done with Art, not wanting to believe he was being unfaithful until confronted by irrefutable evidence?

One thing she knew, she wasn't going to lie to herself any longer. She loved Zephyr. Irrevocably and unequivocally. More than she'd ever loved Art, and she suspected more than she could ever love another person. But if Zephyr could not, or *would not*, love her, then she needed to stop this thing between them before she had no hope of coming out of it with a healable heart.

The thought of letting Zephyr go hurt so badly, an involuntary whimper slipped past her lips. He didn't wake up, but his arms tightened around her, only exacerbating the pain.

Because if she walked away from him, there would be no one there to comfort her.

And that led to her final decision. She wasn't going to waste what might well be her last days with Zephyr as even a pseudo-lover grieving a loss that had not come yet. She would squeeze every bit of joy out of their time together in Greece that she could.

Zephyr woke to the wonderfully pleasant experience of Piper giving him a massage. He was on his stomach, his arms relaxed above his head and his legs stretched out under the light covering of a sheet. She sat on his upper thighs, having an effect on him that he doubted she was going for.

Or maybe not. Piper was the most open and adventurous lover he'd ever had.

It bothered him that her moving him around had not woken him. His ability to incorporate her touch into his dreams showed how deeply he trusted her. As did the secrets of his past he'd shared with her the day before.

He'd never been tempted to tell that story to another woman, and no other lover had been allowed to sleep in his bed, much less wake him with a massage. He'd thought he'd been so clever in pursuing a sexual relationship without strings with the only woman he had ever considered a true friend. Now, he realized that kind of thing led to intimacies he did not crave.

He had to get his relationship with Piper back onto an even keel, or end at least the sexual side of it. Friendship and sex. Nothing more, and certainly nothing so deep it led to true confessions. He'd started at the Plaka, the day before, buying her gifts and clamping down on that dangerous urge to *talk*.

She'd done him a favor waking him with the massage. It would lead to sex and that was something he could handle. He didn't open his mouth to blurt out things better left unsaid when it was busy pleasuring her.

"Mmm…" He stretched under her kneading fingers, rubbing his cheek against the bottom sheet, taking in the scent of their lovemaking from the night before.

Call him earthy, but he loved that smell and often put off their morning shower so he could enjoy it.

"Like that?" Her voice was husky as if she was getting as much out of this as he was.

"Very much. Are you sure you've never gone to massage therapy school?"

"It's one of my many natural talents." Humor laced that sweetly husky voice.

"I admit, I am grateful for this particular talent."

"As you should be. So, I'm the only person in your life with this particular talent?"

"I've never asked Neo if he likes to give massages."

Soft laughter tinkled above him. "I'm having a hard time imagining that conversation."

"You're not the only one."

"There are no other women in your life who know how to relax your muscles like this? I find that hard to believe."

Was she fishing? He'd never asked her if she slept with other men, but he knew she didn't. He didn't make it a habit to sleep with more than one woman at a time, either. It led to messy complications, and he didn't do messy. Though he was rarely with a woman long enough for it to become an issue, he still followed his own rules. His longest liaisons could be measured in months, not years.

"There are no other women in my life, at least none that I would allow in my bed," he amended smartly.

After all, he had as many women working for him as men. Well, maybe not quite as many, but close. There weren't a lot of female construction workers as a percentage overall, especially in countries outside the United States.

She stilled above him. "I'm your only…"

Her words trailed off as if she didn't know how to term herself, and he could not help her. She wasn't a girlfriend per se. She was a friend with whom he shared his body and bed. But it became obvious that she was definitely fishing.

He didn't mind giving her the truth. "I haven't had sex with another woman since the second time we made love."

The first time had scared him shitless and he wasn't afraid to admit it. To himself. But then he'd realized that he was just more physically attracted to Piper than he had been to other women. Add in their friendship and the sex was mind-blowing. He'd decided to enjoy it as long as it lasted.

Because sex never did. Experience had taught him that. Just as it had taught him that while love might be transitory, and family couldn't necessarily be counted on, a true friend stuck with you through the years. He'd learned that from Neo.

Long after the sexual elements to their relationship were over, Zephyr had every expectation that he and Piper would continue to be friends.

"I've never asked for promises of fidelity." She'd gone back to massaging the pleasantly loosening muscles of his lower back.

"And I've never offered them." Because thanks to her ex, she would not believe them. "But if you are asking, I am telling you I don't have sex with other women right now."

"Because of me?"

"Because I have a rule about not having multiple sex partners at the same time," he explained.

"Serial monogamy?"

"Yes. I never make promises, you know that, but while I am having sex with one woman, I do not seek out release elsewhere."

"So, you haven't been with anyone else but me since we started sleeping together."

"Not since the second time, when I knew we would continue to have sex." He'd had a one-night stand after the first time he and Piper had gotten together, when he'd hoped to make their explosive sex a single shot. The hookup had only confirmed that mediocre sex was no substitute for what he had with her right now.

"The first time?"

"Wasn't planned and I wasn't sure we should repeat it."

"But you decided we should?" she asked softly.

"As did you."

"Yes."

"Once I realized you and I were going to have a prolonged sexual association, I stopped looking for that from anyone else." He looked down at her seriously.

"Even when we went weeks between getting together?"

"I don't break my own rules, Piper." He was no oversexed adolescent who could not go a few nights, or weeks, without.

It wasn't always easy, especially when they spoke on the phone and his body reacted with the predictability of Pavlov's dog, but a real man knew how to keep his zipper in the up position. Zephyr was nothing like his father.

Not one damn thing.

"Right." She snorted a laugh.

Pleasure from the massage tried to melt Zephyr's brain along with his muscular tension. "Yes, *right*," he affirmed with emphasis.

But he doubted she believed him, which was why he'd never made promises of fidelity during their temporary sexual relationship. Arthur Bellingham deserved so much more than the small comeuppance Zephyr had engineered for him.

CHAPTER FOUR

"WHAT about you?" he asked, deciding he wanted confirmation of what his instincts told him to be true. "Do you seek sexual release elsewhere when we cannot connect?"

"No." That was decisive enough.

"You made no promises, either," he reminded her.

"No, I didn't, but you're something special. No other man could live up."

"Nice to know." Call him arrogant, but *he* had no trouble believing *her*.

Her hands moved down to his buttocks, digging with her knuckles into his rock-hard glutes.

"Damn." He sighed. "That feels so good."

"I'm enjoying it as much as you are."

"I doubt that." Though he liked hearing it.

"Touching you is always a pleasure." The husky tenor was back in her voice.

Delicious. "Is this touching going to turn sexual?" he could not help hinting.

She scooted down his legs and her fingertips slid between them to caress the back of his balls. "Maybe."

The minx.

He was already hard, but the pressure grew more urgent as her soft touches on his scrotum continued. "You're on dangerous ground there, *pethi mou*."

"Am I?" She was no longer sitting on him, but her knees were still on either side of his.

He took that as an invitation and flipped onto his back, his breath expelling in a hard gust at the sight of her naked body above him. "You are so damn beautiful."

"You're prejudiced."

"You think so, *glyka mou*? I think you could have made millions as a model."

She smiled and shook her head. "Did you just call me sweet?"

"My sweet. You're learning Greek."

"Just that one."

Good. He wasn't sure he wanted her to know he often called her *his woman*. It might sound like he meant something more than he did, but even if their sex wasn't based in some foolish romantic commitment, he was a possessive guy. It was just the way he was made and sometimes, the words *yineka mou* slipped out. She was his, for now. Maybe he should be more circumspect. Now that she was learning what his Greek endearments meant.

His aching hard-on felt ready to explode, distracting him. He gave her his best cajoling look. "Ride me?"

Her stunning blue gaze went dark with passion as he'd known it would. "Do we have time?"

"Always." They were not on a tight schedule, even if she wanted to visit more museums in one day than he usually saw in a year.

She didn't require any more convincing, but moved into position above his bobbing erection. "You look ready to burst."

"I feel it," he choked out gutturally from between clenched teeth as her slick feminine flesh brushed against him.

She went to reach for a condom and he stayed her with a hand between her perfectly shaped breasts. "Neither of us has been with anyone else in almost two years. I've had two clean bills of health over that time."

He knew she'd tested every six months for a couple of years

after finding out Art was such a damn tomcat and wasn't surprised when she said, "Me, too."

"Then, let's go bare." She used the patch for birth control, so they didn't need to worry about making a baby neither of them were ready for.

"Yes," she breathed out, lowering her body so his hard length slid inside her moist channel.

He said that word that she always chided him for and had to fight the urge to surge upward with every ounce of self-control he had earned in his thirty-five years of life. She rewarded his restraint by dropping down and engulfing his entire length in her humid heat. Damn, massaging him *had* excited her.

She was slick with arousal and her inner muscles clenched at him in undeniable need. They moved together like animals mating and yet, not. Their supreme awareness of each other could be no less than human. Their gazes locked and never broke once during the wild ride.

The sensation of their bare skin moving together threw him into a convulsive climax, but he didn't have to worry. She was right there with him, her head thrown back, her pleasure falling from her lips in a keening cry that tingled at the base of his spine.

This moment in time was perfection.

Zephyr surprised himself by enjoying their gluttonous day of museum-viewing. While he liked museums, he wouldn't normally have planned an entire day around visiting as many as he could get to. However, Piper's enthusiasm and fascination was catching. That was the only excuse he could make for how interested he was, even in exhibits that he had seen before as a child on group trips with the other children from the home.

He'd refused to use the term *orphan* because he hadn't been one. He'd had both a mother and a father, even if neither had been willing to make him an important part of their life.

"This just goes to show that we repeat ourselves creatively. This would be considered 'modern art' by current art critics. If it hadn't been dated as being more than four thousand years old."

They were standing in front of an early Cycladic statue that did indeed look like something he might see in a gallery dedicated to modern artists. "It seems odd the statues would be so lacking in intricate detail when the pottery has such complicated patterns on it."

"I'm sure someone hundreds of years from now will find it strange that our houses are built like cookie-cutter images of one another, but we are so particular about what goes inside them."

He turned to her, laying a hand on her waist and not questioning the urge to do so. "You think so?"

"That, or they'll postulate we only ate on plastic because plastic dishes are the only ones that survive that long." Her azure eyes glittered with humor.

"We had stoneware in the home and you're right. It didn't last long."

"My mom bought those unbreakable dishes, but nothing could prevent us kids losing them. The small square bowls made too good a shovel in a pinch."

"I can just imagine you as a small child."

"I was a terror."

"But shy with strangers," he guessed.

"Yep. Teachers never believed my mom about me until I'd organized my first boycott of the cafeteria's no-name catsup. That stuff was nasty. Or had a petition going to reinstate outdoor school when budget cuts threatened that right of passage. It didn't usually happen until my second year in school anyway." She sounded altogether proud of herself.

"I see, you lulled the authority figures around you into complacency and then you sprang."

"That's about it."

He laughed. "I have no problem seeing that."

"Neither did my mother. School administrators were not so insightful." Her eyes twinkled mischeviously. "Until after the fact."

"I shudder to think what your children will be like." Her daughters would be stubborn, her sons protective and both would be intelligent.

She gave him a strange look followed by a negligent shrug that wasn't. Negligent. At least it didn't seem so to him, but he didn't ask her about it because she was already headed to the next display.

She stopped in front of a male kouros statue. "Nice to see Greek men haven't changed in all these millennia."

"I think I'm flattered." The statue had seriously developed abs and thighs that could crack an opponent's back in a wrestling match, ancient or modern. However, the genitals were nothing to write home about. "I hope you are not comparing certain aspects of my anatomy to his understated representation."

She gave him a mocking little smile that made him want to do something that would turn that smile into a grin. "I read somewhere that the aspect of a statue's form was deliberately underrepresented so the focus could be on the aesthetic rather than the sexual."

"That, or the only men willing to be used as artists' models had teeny weenies."

Piper burst out laughing as he'd expected her to, drawing the attention of those around them. While most of it was indulgent, one serious-looking elderly man glared. And a young woman sent daggers Piper's way, but he didn't know if that was for her laughter or the fact she was so clearly with him.

The woman had given him an encouraging once-over when he and Piper had first arrived at the National Museum, but he had ignored her.

Once again, he turned his back on her and smiled down at

his beautiful companion. "That is not something you have to worry about in my bed, no?"

"You, Zephyr Nikos, are a braggart. And a bad, bad man." The laughter still laced her voice and he wanted to kiss its flavor from her lips, but he refrained.

Stealing a kiss at the Acropolis, he could get away with. But he'd get more than one glare at such a public display of affection in the National Museum. Greece was not America, or even England for that matter, when it came to love affairs being conducted in public. It was generally a far more conservative country.

That had never bothered him before, but he wanted to kiss his *yineka*. However, he refused to embarrass her.

He would make up for it and then some when they returned to their room later.

The next morning, Piper tried to gather her thoughts as hot water pelted down over her during her solitary shower. The day before, they'd both admitted to fidelity and agreed to stop using condoms. She'd wanted the illusion of deeper intimacy for what she was coming to accept would have to be their last tryst and had readily agreed.

Only later had she begun to wonder if those were the actions of a man who would never love her? At first, she'd discounted his assertion he hadn't been with another woman since the second time they'd made love, but as the day wore on she'd asked herself why. And she hadn't liked the answer. She would not let Art have that much control of her present, regardless of how his betrayal had hurt.

But even believing in Zephyr's faithfulness, what did that mean? Was he capable of loving her? So many things pointed to a yes answer, even as his self-admissions denied the possibility.

Their time at the museums had been almost magical, full of laughter and subtle marks of affection between them. The little touches had added up and by the time they returned to their hotel to get ready for dinner, Zephyr had overcome her with a storm of desire. They'd missed their reservations and had a local café deliver dinner to their room.

Zephyr had been right when asked. For enough money, any restaurant *would* deliver food to a hungry couple. Even a couple who had refused to leave their hotel room while sating a different hunger than that of the stomach.

How could she end their sexual liaison without ending their friendship? Did she have enough strength of will to be his friend without falling back into his bed? And even if she did, would maintaining their friendship be the best thing for her emotional well-being? How was she going to get over him if she continued to see him?

But how could she stop seeing him without totally shattering what was left of her heart?

This morning had only added to her already roiling thoughts and emotions. They'd once again made love and it had been so profound, she'd been a breath away from blurting out her love for him.

She'd needed some time to get her emotions back under control and insisted Zephyr take one of his military-length showers. Alone. He often bragged about the quick grooming habits he'd learned on the ship he'd worked when leaving Greece and she wasn't above playing to that pride. She'd used the excuse that they needed to get going if they were going to make it to the seaside village that was home to Trident's temple ruins in time to actually see them.

Clearly indulging her, he'd agreed. And she'd gotten a few precious and necessary minutes to herself, both while he showered and now while she did.

The only problem was, her emotions were just as raw now as they had been while she and Zephyr made love. She ached with the need to tell him of her feelings, but was afraid that they would be an unwelcome burden. And she couldn't squash the hope that maybe if he just realized it was safe to love her, that she wouldn't betray him as others had in the past, he might let his heart out of its self-imposed prison.

Carefully, she swiped soapy hands over her birth control patch. Or rather where the patch was supposed to be.

No. No, no, no, no.

It was there. It had to be. She craned her neck over her shoulder to look down at her right hip, but saw nothing except smooth skin. She looked over the other side, praying she'd forgotten that she'd used a different hip this time. But no flesh-colored square resided there, either.

Where was it? She wasn't due to replace the weekly dose of birth control until the day after tomorrow and she wasn't scheduled to be without until a full week after that.

Oh, God. The prayer left her lips in desperation as she tried to remember the last time she'd checked the patch.

Having it there had become such second nature that she barely even noticed it anymore. She was always careful in the shower, never soaping the area directly. She'd lost one the first month she was using them, but she'd soon learned how to avoid corrupting the adhesive that held the hormone dispenser in place.

She forced her mind to bring up and scour images from the preceding days, but the last clear impression she had of her patch was during her shower in a Midwest hotel room the morning before catching her flight to Greece. No, she couldn't have lost it her first day in Athens.

It wouldn't have just fallen off. But the way she and Zephyr had touched that first time making love after their weeks-long separation had been rough, urgent and not at all careful of clothing, much less an adhesive square attached to her body. But if she'd lost it *then*, they had made love a number of times since without *any* form of protection.

Her breath choked in her throat at the very real possibility of what that could mean. No. She refused to believe God would be that cruel.

She felt like hyperventilating as she asked herself what to do now. How was she supposed to walk away from Zephyr if she was pregnant with his child? Would he believe that she had not done it on purpose? Losing the condoms had been his idea, but would he remember that when faced with the unexpected results?

She didn't want to tell him pregnancy was even a possibility. Doing so would only add stress between them when there was as much a chance she wasn't now carrying new life as that she was. Maybe even more so, considering how long she'd been on the patch.

However, if she didn't tell him, how would she explain the need to return to using condoms? Also, if she didn't, how would she ever be able to explain that level of dishonesty to herself? A lie of omission was still a lie, wasn't it?

She wanted Zephyr to believe it was safe to love her, that he could trust her with his deepest emotions and needs. How could she build that trust with him if she hid something this important from him? Wasn't it better to be honest and up-front about what was going on, rather than pretending everything was fine when it very much was not?

Hadn't Art done that to her? And before him, her parents? Who often waited until the last possible moment to warn her about the next move? They'd always justified this behavior by saying they had enough to deal with without her and her brother and sister having a month-long temper tantrum about leaving their friends behind. They gave just enough time for their children to say goodbye to their closest friends before uprooting them for her father's newest military assignment.

Certainty and something like a fatalistic dread settled inside her. Though maybe for the first time, she began to understand her parents' thinking; she wasn't about to play that kind of game with Zephyr.

She quickly finished her shower, dressed and pulled her hair into an easy ponytail, rather than styling it. She bypassed makeup and exited the en suite bathroom a good ten minutes ahead of schedule.

Zephyr was just closing the door behind their room-service delivery. He turned to her with a sexy smile. "Breakfast is served."

"Perfect." Should she tell him now, or wait until later?

"You look a little shaken," he said with a frown of concern. "Did you see a spider in the shower, or something?"

"Please. I'm not even a little arachnophobic." But *shaken* described nicely how she felt.

"That's good to know."

"Yes, well, um…"

He stopped uncovering dishes and stared at her, his concern obviously amping up a notch. "You're starting to worry me."

"That might be wise. To be worried, I mean. Though, honestly, they say it takes positively months to get pregnant after you stop using birth control usually." Oh, man, she was making a cake of this, a very messy one. "There's no reason to assume tragic consequences now."

"What are you talking about?" He stopped, going absolutely still. "Did you say *pregnant*? You're on the birth control patch."

"Yes, I would be, if it was actually there, I mean. If I had it on."

"Of course it's on. You *never* forget it." He was starting to look a little shaken himself.

"I didn't forget it this time, but it's not there."

"Not there?" Six feet three inches of solid muscle went boneless and he dropped to sit on the chair behind him. Hard. "Your…my…you…I…"

"You sound as coherent as I felt when I first realized it was gone." Truth was, she wasn't feeling that much better right now.

He stared off into space for several seconds and then shook his head. "I don't remember seeing it." He leaned on the table with his elbows, his head in his hands. "I don't remember seeing it, but I wasn't looking, either."

"Since that first time day before yesterday?"

"I wouldn't have noticed anything then. But no, not since." He looked at her with an expression she'd never seen on the big tycoon's face. Fear coupled with guilt. Severe guilt. "*I never even noticed.* Can you forgive me?"

Okay, that was not expected. She'd anticipated anger, blame, even horror, but not an obviously genuine guilt-fueled apology.

She crossed the room and dropped to her knees in front of him, putting her hands on his thighs. "It's not your fault. I didn't notice it was gone, either. We were, um…busy, in the shower yesterday and I'm just so used to it being there, I never even thought to check."

"But you checked today."

"More like I noticed when I went to wash that area more carefully."

"I cannot believe I did not pay closer attention. And then I asked you to stop using condoms." His voice dripped with agonized culpability.

Okay, so she definitely did not have to worry about him blaming her, but she didn't want him feeling guilty, or like an idiot. Even if she did. "We're both adults. We *both* didn't realize. The patch was my responsibility."

"That is like saying that remembering to use a condom was my purview alone and I know you did not see it that way."

"It's not the same thing."

"Of course it is. Besides, sharing the blame does no good and makes no difference to the child we may have created."

"There's no reason to assume I'm pregnant." That was one leap of faith she did not want to make right now. "I told you, many women take months to get pregnant after they stop using the patch."

"You also called possible pregnancy a tragedy." He didn't look very happy about that. At all. "You would not consider termination?"

"What? No, definitely not. That would never be an option for me."

He looked relieved, but no happier. "Still, you consider the possible consequences *tragic*."

"I didn't mean that. Not really. I'm frightened of what this would mean for me, for us, if I were pregnant," she admitted, emotion choking her.

"I am neither of my parents. You understand?" He said something in Greek she had no hope of understanding, then gave her a look she wouldn't want to see across a boardroom or in a dark alley for that matter. *"I will not abandon my child."*

That was one thing she would never have worried about, even if he hadn't said it. Then a way of getting him off this line of enquiry came to her. "I would never expect you to, but could we please stop talking like pregnancy is a foregone conclusion?"

"And you?" he asked, clearly ignoring her plea.

She tried not to be offended he had even asked. In his mind, he had good reason for doing so. Irrefutable experience. But still, the question hurt. "I'm not your mother. I don't have to give my child up in order to leave a soul-destroying life behind."

"How long since your last period?"

"What, are you an expert on menstrual cycles?" she challenged.

"No."

"I'm not, either." She blew out a frustrated breath. "But I do know somewhere in the middle of your cycle is the most likely time for pregnancy to occur."

"And?"

She winced, wishing she could say something else. "I'm pretty much smack-dab there right now."

"Even so, as you say, many women do not fall pregnant quickly after being on birth control for a prolonged period. How long have you been on the patch?"

"I started taking it with Art and never went off, even though

I was celibate until that first time with you. I liked the way it balanced my monthly hormone cycle."

"That is a significant amount of time."

"Yes."

"So, the chances you are pregnant are diminished?"

"So I've been led to believe." She looked at him worriedly.

"But diminished is not nonexistent."

"No."

"Are you very angry?"

"Angry? No. Well, maybe a smidge with myself. I feel like an idiot for not keeping more attentive track, especially when we stopped using condoms."

"But you are not angry at the prospect of carrying my child?"

"No." Oh, heck. She might as well go for broke. She was feeling reckless and tired of hiding feelings that were so strong they left little room for anything else. "I can't imagine anyone I would rather have as the father of my child."

Shock froze his features for several long seconds. "You do not mean that."

"I don't lie."

"No, you don't. No more than I."

That was something she still had to work on believing, but she wasn't going to tell him that. Because *Zephyr* had never done anything to earn her mistrust.

"I guess a billionaire real-estate tycoon would make an admirable choice as father for your child," he said in his second full-scale departure from tact.

She *just* managed to stop herself clouting him. "This is more of that, *they want me in their life for what I can buy for them garbage*, isn't it? I don't look at you as a meal ticket, Zee."

And he'd better get that through his head right now, or they were going to have more problems between them than an un-anticipated possible pregnancy.

He jolted. "You have never called me that before."

Sometimes, he focused on the least important things.

"I've heard Neo do so." But he was right. For some reason, believing she might be pregnant with Zephyr's child made her feel more comfortable with the casual intimacy.

"Yes."

"If you don't like it, I won't do it again," she offered.

"I do not mind."

"Fine. Um, we need to make a plan."

"You need to eat breakfast." Again with the non sequitur, but maybe that was okay. For now.

She needed some time to think if nothing else. "So do you."

"Then let us eat." And incredibly, they managed to do that without any further discussion of possible consequences of the lack of birth control.

They were halfway to Sounion before he mentioned the morning's disturbing revelations again.

"So, a plan," he said as they drove down the coastal highway.

"We should, um, probably go back to using condoms until we know if I'm pregnant." She had realized during her personal ruminations that was as far as she wanted to go with contingency arrangements at present. Her mind simply refused to wrap around the prospect of a child. Their baby. Growing inside her body.

Yesterday, she'd been thinking she had to tell him goodbye once and for all and now she was faced with the prospect of never being able to do so, even if they stopped making love.

"Yes."

"I don't want to put another patch on, just in case, even though it is not likely, but we should definitely use condoms." She shook her head at herself. She didn't want to risk hurting a baby that probably didn't even exist.

"You've mentioned that point several times."

"Have I?"

"Yes."

"I'm sorry," she apologized distractedly.

"Are you that disturbed by the idea of being pregnant with my child?"

"We've already covered this ground."

"Then by the prospect of being pregnant at all?" He slid a sidelong glance at her before looking back at the road.

"I'm building a business. Having a baby will change a lot of things, including how much time I can spend on work." It was the only concern she was willing to voice right this second. She'd been on an emotional thrill ride since discovering the loss of her patch. Fear competed with hope and illicit joy at the prospect in equal measure.

"And this worries you?"

"A little," she admitted. "I'm willing to rearrange my priorities though. Any child of mine will not pay for the choices of its parents."

"As you felt you paid for yours." He saw immediately her determination to give her child everything she felt she'd missed out on.

"To an extent, but even more so, as you paid for yours."

"I cannot disagree there." He smiled grimly.

"I'm not asking you to."

"That is good."

"I hate this," she cried out on an explosive breath.

"What?"

"How stilted we are with each other. We were closer than we'd ever been and now this."

"We are friends," he said, frowning. "You being pregnant with my child will not change that."

"We are more than friends, Zee. At least give me that much." So, maybe she did want to deal with something besides the condom issue.

"What do you mean?"

"Don't play dumb. It's unbecoming, not to mention lacking in credibility."

"I am not playing at anything." He sounded offended, his

voice sliding into that zone she'd come to recognize as his anger. The chill-factor was definitely in evidence.

"I'm sorry." She stared out the window, blinking back tears she couldn't even name the exact reason for. "I don't mean to patronize you."

"Thank you."

"Somewhere along the way, we stopped being merely friends with benefits. I mean, for me anyway."

"You prefer the term *lovers*?" he asked.

"That would be a start." Not everything she wanted, but a definite beginning.

"But lovers are never permanent in my life." Worry crept back into his voice, letting her know this was a genuine concern on his part.

"Make me the exception."

"I do not know if I can do that." He sighed. "Though if you are pregnant, neither of us will have a choice."

The next-to-last thing she wanted was to be in his life by default. The last thing was to be out of his life completely, which said what about her plans to walk away from what they had before she got even more hurt? "I don't want it to be that way."

"What we want is not always what we get."

She thought of the many times she'd had to move away from friends and activities that meant something to her. Then she remembered how helpless she had felt in the face of her ex-husband's unrepentant and repeated infidelity. "That's only too true."

He took a deep breath and let it out with a big smile somewhere between appearing genuine and his game face. "So, let us forget for today that you might be pregnant with my child."

"And on the verge of losing my dreams? Okay, I can do that."

His jaw went taut, but he let her flippancy go. "Good. We will go to Sounion and play tourists and then catch the helicopter there as planned and fly to the island early this evening."

"Will we make love tonight?"

"Did you want to make an appointment?" he teased.

"I just want to know that you haven't already decided you are bored with me."

"How can you even suggest that?"

"You're the one who said…you know what, never mind. Let's just focus on the present. Not the past. Not the future and definitely not the possibility we've started on that dynasty of yours earlier than expected." Not to mention with a woman he hadn't considered in the running for mother of his children a mere forty-eight hours ago.

"Right."

And somehow, they managed it. Though she had to give most of the credit to Zephyr. Every time she started to worry, he seemed to know…and knew exactly how to stop it.

CHAPTER FIVE

FROM the air, the view of Zephyr and Neo's newest acquisition was incredible. Piper had no problem imagining this small Greek island as an oasis for the resort's guests. Unlike many of the rocky islands that dotted the sea off the coastline of mainland Greece, this landscape was covered with lush grasses and green trees. There was a large olive grove and what looked like a citrus orchard.

They flew over the fishing village, traditional white houses with red roofs showing where the year-round residents lived. The boats that bobbed in the water, moored to the long dock, looked picturesque in their simplicity. No fancy trawlers here.

A tan circle painted with white directional lines about two hundred yards from a large villa set atop a cliff overlooking the sea had to be their landing destination. Piper shouldn't have been surprised that a family who at one time had the wherewithal to own an island had installed a helipad on it. Only, she was. She would have expected a landing strip for small planes and said as much to Zephyr on the walk to the villa.

A young man who introduced himself as the housekeeper's grandson insisted on carrying their luggage in a yard cart.

"The patriarch preferred travel by sea, but his children insisted on faster transportation to the mainland," Zephyr replied in response to her comment. "As to why it was a helicopter over a jet, I could not say. I think he balked at the excavation necessary for a flat runway long enough to service a jet."

"We'll be doing that excavation, won't we? I mean guests are going to want to be able to fly in."

The young man leading the way with his cart looked back at her, his expression troubled.

Zephyr did not seem to notice, but he shook his head in negation. "The focus of the spa resort is going to be total relaxation. It will start with a luxury yacht ride from the mainland."

"I bet you'll stick with helicopters." But she would have enjoyed a decadent ride on a yacht.

Zephyr shrugged. "I am not a prospective guest."

"Maybe you should be."

"Perhaps you should as well. We can attend the grand opening week together," he said as he reached out to open the front door, only to have it swing inward before he touched it.

An elderly Greek woman welcomed them inside before shooting rapid-fire instructions at her grandson, who took his cart around to the side of the villa.

"The young, they forget the proprieties," she said in perfect English, if accented charmingly. She shook her head. "Maybe that one *should* be a fisherman."

"There will be many jobs for those willing to work both building the resort and working there after it is completed."

"You will give first chance to locals?" the old woman asked with obvious hope.

"Yes," Zephyr said decisively. "We do not want the year-round residents to feel disconnected to the resort. Their participation in the venture is essential."

Her lined visage wreathed with a smile, the housekeeper led them into an oversized sitting room with a truly impressive view. The wall facing the sea had such large windows it felt like it was made of glass.

"Would you like refreshments?" she asked.

"Your former employer rhapsodized about the fresh lemonade made from local fruit."

Appearing pleased by the request, the housekeeper nodded. "I will send a girl with a tray."

"Thank you. Has Mr. Tilieu been told of our arrival?" Zephyr asked.

"He has, though how anyone could miss the sound of a landing helicopter, I do not know."

Piper stifled a grin, while Zephyr obviously bit back a smile.

"I take it you prefer to travel by boat?" Piper asked.

"I prefer not to travel at all, but how others can stand to ride in those noisy things is a mystery to me." The gray-haired woman waved her hands in dismissal.

"Sometimes needs must," Zephyr said wryly.

"As you say, Kyrie Nikos." Then she left.

He turned to Piper. "Beautiful, isn't it?"

"Absolutely gorgeous." She didn't even try to resist the lure of huge picture windows. "I could spend hours just looking out these windows."

He came to stand beside her, close but not touching. "It is mesmerizing. The sunset will be spectacular."

"Will we be able to watch it?"

"If that is your desire."

"You've been very indulgent with me this trip." Though since sharing his past with her, he had maintained a distance even his charm could not hide. Their discovery this morning had not altered that distance, despite other small changes in his behavior.

"You deserve a little spoiling."

"I won't complain about you thinking so."

"Good." He shifted beside her and she could feel his regard transferring to her from the view. "Speaking of being spoiled, do you want to attend the opening week with me?"

"I have no doubt you'll be here for the grand opening, but I sincerely doubt it will be for the rest and relaxation the resort is going to offer."

"I will make sure you are still pampered," he assured her.

"What about you?"

"What about me?" he asked, not following.

"Don't you think you could do with a bit of pampering?"

"I will avail myself of the spa services."

"To check their quality standard, I bet."

"So?"

"So, you're something of a workaholic," she clarified.

"As are you."

"I love my business." But she wasn't really a workaholic. Once her business was established, she had every intention of cutting back her hours to make room for other things. "I never intended it to be everything in my life."

"Then why do you consider the prospect of parenting the dissolution of your dreams?"

Shocked at his interpretation of her earlier words, she jerked in startlement. "I didn't mean my business."

He didn't look like he believed her. "What did you mean, then?"

"It's not something I want to discuss right now." Really. Truly. It would do neither of them any good to hash over her old dream of building a life with a man who loved her, and the more recently acknowledged dream of having Zephyr be that loving man.

He opened his mouth to say something, but before he got a chance, a masculine voice from behind them said, "You've arrived. Finally."

They both turned to face an attractive black man.

Zephyr stepped forward with his hand out. "Ah, Jean-René. Good to see you."

He turned back to Piper. "*Pethi mou*, this is our architect, Jean-René Tilieu. Jean-René, this is Piper Madison, our designer."

Jean-René's smile was white-white and full of charm as he bent over Piper's extended hand, rather than shaking it. "An exceptional pleasure, mademoiselle."

"*Merci*. I'm really looking forward to working with you. I find your work both inspiring and impressive."

"Ah, you know the way to a man's heart is flattery, *non*?"

Zephyr stepped forward and put his arm around Piper's waist. "Piper does not flatter, she always speaks the truth."

Jean-René gave them a speculative look and then met her eyes, his expression serious. "Then I am doubly honored by your praise, mademoiselle."

"Piper, please."

"That is an interesting name, *n'est-ce pas*?"

"I was named for one of my father's mentors in the army," she informed him.

Zephyr looked down at her. "You never told me that."

"It's a bit embarrassing, to be named after a grizzled army master sergeant who chewed tobacco and shot pistols with equal enthusiasm."

"Piper is a feminine name, though, *non*? This master sergeant who chewed tobacco is a woman?" Jean-René asked.

Piper laughed. "No, *Pipes* is his nickname and I never asked how he got it."

"That's probably best," Zephyr said, humor lacing his tone.

She smiled up at him. "That's what I thought."

"Two great minds." Jean-René flashed that brilliant smile again. "Clearly this project is in sympathetic hands."

"Without a doubt. I've studied your work in depth and I've worked on enough developments with Zephyr to know that our approaches are going to dovetail nicely." Her only concern, and it was not strong, was how the Greek contractor would be to work with as he was a complete unknown to her.

"*Très bien*. Do you wish to discuss initial thoughts over dinner, or wait until tomorrow?" he asked Zephyr.

Zephyr turned his head so his and Piper's gazes met. "What do you think?"

Why was he asking her? Maybe this was about watching the sunset. "Is the dining room on this side of the house?"

"No, but we can eat in here," Zephyr replied.

"*Mais oui*, the view of the setting sun is *magnifique*. I saw the most glorious rays yesterday evening when I arrived."

"Then it is settled." She stepped away from both men and headed toward the stairs. "I'm happy to jump right in, as I'm sure you are both eager to do. Which room is mine?"

"I had the housekeeper put us in the master suite." This time Zephyr did not ask her opinion and his expression dared her to disagree.

Like she was going to argue. She *enjoyed* sleeping with him. "I'll see you upstairs, then."

She went in search of the master suite, assuming it wouldn't be difficult to find and she was right. The fact that she found a maid inside unpacking their cases was almost as big a clue as the giant four-poster bed that would have looked silly anywhere *but* a master bedroom.

It was covered with a cotton spread in eggshell-white, decorated with intricate stitching a single shade darker. Gauze curtains draped the bed, the large picture window and the French doors leading out onto the second-story balcony that wrapped around the house. The armoire, dresser and matching bedside tables were heavy wooden pieces, stained dark. It was easy to tell that this had been a man's room, but she still liked it. A lot.

Taking in the gorgeous view, she skimmed off the royal-blue shortwaisted jacket she'd donned over a paler blue sheath dress that morning. She tossed it over the back of one of the twin oversized armchairs. They faced a large stone fireplace that was laid for a fire.

Interesting. If the weather leant itself toward doing so, she would want to talk to Jean-René about incorporating fireplaces in the main areas of the resort at least.

"Pardon me, but do you speak English?" she asked the maid, who was now sliding their cases under the huge bed and out of the way.

"Yes."

"Great, because my Greek is nonexistent."

The young woman smiled. "You are American, yes?"

"Yes. I took Spanish in school." It was the only language she knew she would find at any high school, no matter where her father had been stationed, so she could take it for the full four years. "Will it get cold enough in the evenings to light the fire?"

"Some, yes. Not so cold, but the fire, it is cozy."

"I see." Piper smiled. "Thank you."

"You are welcome."

"When did Mr. Nikos give instructions for us to share a room?" She felt ridiculous asking, but *needed* the answer for some reason.

The maid gave her an odd look, but didn't hesitate to answer. "I do not know. On Monday, the housekeeper, she tell me to ready the room for Kyrie Nikos and his guest."

So, he'd planned to share a room all along. This was not altogether shocking. They did not take pains to hide their sexual relationship, but he was not usually so blatant in a work setting. Before his revelations over dinner in Athens, she would have taken this as a good sign for the future of their relationship.

Now, it just added to her confusion about the man she loved.

Prior to this morning, he had not considered her in the role of mother to his children. He had also made it clear he did not anticipate ever entering into a permanent relationship with her. All bets were off if she was pregnant, though. That was something she had no doubts about.

If she was carrying his baby, he would insist on marriage. His assertion he was nothing like his parents hadn't been necessary for her to realize Zephyr Nikos would insist on being a major player in his child's life.

She just wasn't sure what *she* wanted to do about that.

Zephyr found Piper sitting on a cushioned wrought-iron lounger on the terrace outside their bedroom. "Tired, *pethi mou*?"

"What?" She looked up at him, eyes the same color as the sea they'd been gazing at vague. "No. I was just thinking, trying to work things out and getting more confused in the process."

"Would you like a sounding board?"

"Not this time."

He frowned; that was not the answer he wanted, he realized. "You like the house?"

"You know I do. But *house*? I don't think so. *Mansion* more like. How many bedrooms does this place have anyway?"

"Twelve, four of them large suites like this one."

"Then how can you tell this is the master?" she challenged him.

"How did you tell?"

"The maid was unpacking our cases."

"Really, that was it?" One eyebrow raised knowingly.

"You know it wasn't."

He nodded. "The bed."

"It couldn't be in any room but the master."

"Exactly." He moved to stand in front of her and put a hand out, which she automatically took. "I'm glad we aren't tearing it down." Sometimes, they had no choice but to destroy in order to build something new. Thankfully, that was not necessary this time.

"Is it going to be part of the resort?" Piper asked, not looking all that pleased at the prospect.

He tugged her to stand, then took her place in the chair and pulled her into his lap. "At first, I thought it would, but every time I come, I grow more attached to the place. Neo likes it as well. I think we may keep it for our personal use, but he'll have to find his own master-suite bed, I'm keeping this one."

"Really?"

"Why so surprised? We agreed the bed is perfect."

"That's not what I meant." She squirmed until she was comfortable against him, having a predictable effect on the blood-flow south of his waist. "I don't see either of you relaxing enough to get any use out of it."

"He's getting married. They will have children. This is a good place to bring them. The resort will only make it better. Cass likes to travel, but prefers private residence to hotels."

"That makes sense, considering."

"Yes." He tugged her to relax further against his chest. "And you, can you imagine staying here on the occasional holiday?"

She sighed, her head coming to rest against his shoulder. "Too easily. If I owned a property like this, I wouldn't relegate it to vacation home, though. I couldn't resist living here." The buried longing in her voice surprised him. "I don't know how the previous owners did."

"How would you run your business from here?"

"I thought daydreams didn't have to be practical."

"Indulge me." He wrapped his arms around her waist, enjoying this moment of relaxed closeness.

She was good for him, which was just the dangerous kind of thinking he needed to avoid before he started spilling secrets again. This was about learning what was going on in her complicated brain, not revealing more of his own thoughts. And he would remember that.

"Living here would be the ultimate indulgence, but in answer to your all too prosaic question, with high-speed Internet, a reliable telephone service and a color fax machine, I could run my business from anywhere."

"It would require a lot of travel." Especially if she continued to work full-time.

"I travel a lot now."

Didn't he know it? He understood her desire to live here, though. "I forget how much I enjoy the sunshine sometimes, but a few days in Greece and I'm spoiled to blue skies again."

"We can't claim our fair share of those in Seattle." She gave a rueful sigh.

He chuckled. "This is true. The first year Neo and I lived there, we thought the rain would never end."

"Seattle gets all four seasons."

"And all of them have rain."

"True," she said grudgingly. "But it's better than New York blizzards, trust me."

"Here, though, the weather is perfect." He and Neo had not left Greece because they wanted to get away from the sunshine.

"If you are partial to a warm climate."

"Which I am."

"Me, too." She sighed. "Maybe I should have relocated to Southern California, when I left New York."

"No, we would not have met."

"You might have been better off."

What? He did not think so. He maneuvered her so their gazes met, and saw that her azure eyes were troubled. He shook his head. "Are you trying to imply that our friendship has been a detriment to me in some way?"

"Well, it's not as if I'm the woman you envisioned as the mother of your future children." Her voice echoed with pain he would not have expected.

"I had not given any thought to who that might be." No serious contemplation anyway. He had thought of her in that role, before they started having sex. He admired her character and thought she would make an ideal mother and wife, except for that romantic streak even her rotten marriage had not cured her of.

"But you would not have considered me."

"You are right." At least that had been his final determination.

She turned her head away completely, but not before he saw sadness making her blue eyes shimmer dangerously.

Oh, no. Tears were not going to happen. He gently, but inexorably, tugged her face back around. "Not because I do not think you would be eminently suitable, but because I knew you would never consider a…what did you call my nebulous marriage plans? *A business merger*."

"Why would it have to be a business transaction between the two of us?" she asked plaintively.

"How could it be anything else?"

"Love."

"Love?" Hadn't they already discussed this? "Whatever propensity to love I may have had once is gone. Even if it were not, love does not always last. Blood ties do not count for much, either."

"So, there is nothing left but business?"

"True friendship can endure," he admitted.

"Like your friendship with Neo."

"Yes."

"He's the only person in your life who has never let you down, isn't he?"

"On a personal level? Yes." He brushed her lips with his thumb. "Well, not actually. You have never let me down, either."

"Until this morning." Her lower lip trembled and she bit it.

"You did not let me down."

"How can you say that?" she asked.

"It is the truth. We are done assigning blame, remember?"

"I don't think I got the memo." She gave a pale version of her usual teasing smile, but at least she was no longer on the verge of tears.

He hoped. "We agreed this morning."

"That was not agreement, that was you saying it did no good."

"I am right."

"You have what can be an annoying tendency to think you are." But she nuzzled his neck and he was not too worried.

"What can I say? I usually am."

She pulled back and gave him a gloating glare. "Ah, so you admit to at least some small level of infallibility."

"Naturally."

"You're so darn arrogant." She shook her head in bemusement. "Why do I find that charming again?"

"You tell me."

"I plead the Fifth."

"We are in Greece," Zephyr pointed out, "not the U.S. The Fifth Amendment does not apply here."

"I bet the Greek constitution has some similar guarantee against having to testify against themselves for their citizens."

"We are getting off topic here."

"You're right." Piper gathered her thoughts. "Why, if you trust friendship so much, do you think a marriage based on it would fail?"

"I did not say I believed a marriage between us would fail utterly, but it *would* fail to make you happy." And ultimately, that had decided him against the prospect.

"Why? Would you plan to sleep around after?"

"No. I could give you fidelity." Of that, he had no doubts. "However, I could not give you something you've made clear is of equal importance to you." Long before their discussion of love at dinner the other night, he had known she was still waiting for her fairy-tale ending complete with love ever after and Prince Charming.

He was a former street rat, no prince, and love was not, and never would be, on his agenda.

"You're talking about love again, aren't you?"

"Yes. Can you honestly say you would have considered a marriage proposal without it?"

She bit her lip and looked away, shaking her head once in negation.

"As I thought."

"So, where does that leave us?"

"I do not know." If she was pregnant with his child, he would try to convince her to accept his proposal, regardless of her finer feelings.

He knew his inner ruthlessness would show itself and he could not even be sorry about that. If she carried his baby, neither of their dreams took precedence. They would do what was best for their child.

He would never allow a child of his to be anything but absolutely certain of its place in his life. Unlike both his mother and father, Zephyr Nikos would consider his role as parent the most important one he would ever hold.

He did not know how to be a father, but he and Neo had self-educated themselves in business and that had been an eminently successful endeavor. With the same work and dedication, he could learn how to be a dad as well. Unlike when he was a teenager, he did not have to rely on used books, and firsthand experience at ground level.

He could afford to consult the most eminent minds in the field of child development, read the best books on the subject and do whatever else was necessary to be the best parent possible.

Zephyr had never done things by halves and becoming a parent would be no exception.

"I don't want to take an over-the-counter pregnancy test," Piper said after several quiet moments of her head resting on his shoulder again.

"So, we will wait until we return to Seattle and make an appointment with your doctor. We are only scheduled to be here three days."

"They'll feel like an eternity."

He could not disagree.

The contractor arrived the next morning and between the four of them, they kept extremely busy laying the groundwork for preliminary plans to be drawn up. Jean-René flirted shamelessly with Piper, making her smile when that worried expression slid into her eyes.

Zephyr did not worry about the other man, knowing he adored his French wife and would never consider betraying her. Besides, Zephyr had made it patently clear that he and Piper were together.

On their last night, they climbed the stairs after a lively postdinner discussion over whether or not to place the main resort near the current villa, or nearer the accessible beach on the northern shore of the island. Piper was in favor of the beach, but the contractor liked the idea of taking advantage of already existing power and water access.

Jean-René had played devil's advocate, arguing both for and against each of the locations.

Zephyr had made the final decision, going with the beach-front scenario. Guests would appreciate the easy access to the ocean and while the view might not be quite as majestic, it was still magnificent. Besides, it would give him and Neo and their future families privacy when they were on the island.

"You know he reminds me a little of Art, only different," Piper said.

"The contractor?"

"Jean-René. He flirts. All the time, but there is no sexual heat behind it."

"And there was with Art."

"Yes. He accused me of being immaturely jealous, but after seeing Jean-René in action, I can say definitely that the intent behind the flirting makes all the difference."

"Yes, Jean-René is a Frenchman. He flirts with a ninety-year-old grandmother as warmly as he would a runway model."

Piper nodded. "It's all about making a woman smile, without making her feel like sexual prey."

"Art did not understand the difference?"

"How could he? Any woman even halfway attractive to him *was* sexual prey." The disgust that tinged Piper's tone was a definite improvement over the grief that used to lie so heavily on her when she talked about her ex.

"*I* do not flirt." Or rather, he only flirted with intent and since he and Piper had begun their liaison, there had been no other woman he wished to seduce.

She laughed and hugged him, right there on the stairs. "No, you don't."

He enjoyed the spontaneous embrace. While she never

drew away from his displays of affection, she had been more circumspect in offering her own since they reached the villa. He didn't know if that was because she blamed him for her possible pregnancy, though she'd said she didn't. Or maybe she was responding to his pulling away from talking about personal things.

He just did not see the need to discuss their future when they did not know whether they needed to take a pregnancy into account, or not. He'd also resisted talking any more about his past. It was over and done. They did not need to keep revisiting it.

He followed her into the bedroom and closed the door behind them. "Are you ready to go back to Seattle tomorrow?"

Drawing aside the drape at the window, she did not answer for several seconds. "I don't know."

"It is hard to leave here." He began divesting himself of his clothes.

"But I want to know."

He did not ask what she wanted to know. There was only one thing causing worry lines between her elegant brows.

Part of him, a very large part if he were honest with himself, *wanted* her to be pregnant. Then he could be selfish and convince her to marry him despite the lack of love between them. It would be the best thing for the baby and he trusted her to make the needs of her child paramount.

He cupped her shoulder, caressing her nape with his thumb. "I have something more interesting to focus on than a dark vista."

She turned to face him, her expression soft and yearning. "Do you?"

"Can you doubt it?"

She just shook her head and waited. Waited for him to kiss her, to touch her, to show her that in this at least, they had perfection.

And that was exactly what he did.

* * *

Piper flew back to Seattle in Zephyr's private jet with him. When they landed, she learned that he had already made an appointment for the next morning with her doctor. She wasn't even a little surprised by his excessive efficiency. She was a bit startled by the fact that he'd gotten an appointment so quickly. She was never so lucky with her doctor's appointment keeper.

But then Zephyr Nikos moved entire ranges, not simply single mountains, when he wanted to.

He spent the night with Piper in her apartment. They didn't make love that night, but he held her close in the darkness protecting her dreams and making her feel safe.

"We'll call you tomorrow with the results," the nurse said after setting the vial with Piper's blood aside.

Piper stood up and put the chair they'd used for the blood draw back against the wall at the head of the exam table. "Thank you. Have the doctor call my cell phone, all right?"

"Of course. I don't think our office has ever successfully gotten hold of you on your house or business line."

"I travel a lot."

"It must be nice." The nurse put the vial in a small red carrier.

"It can be." When she'd first moved to Seattle, she'd loved the travel, but after she and Zephyr became friends, she missed him when she was away. Even before the sexual side to their relationship started. "It can be exhausting, too."

"Well, if this test comes back positive, you can count on being exhausted even more." The wry grimace on the usually friendly nurse's face could in no way be described as a smile.

What was she supposed to say to that? Thank you? She was sure the other woman thought her information necessary, if not welcome. Piper would rather focus on the upside of this pregnancy…just as soon as she figured it out. She got up and grabbed her bag. "Well, um…goodbye."

"See you soon."

Piper didn't know about that. She rarely visited her doctor between physicals. Of course, if she was pregnant, that would have to change, wouldn't it?

CHAPTER SIX

ZEPHYR was waiting for her when she came out. "How did it go?"

"A little prick, a bandage and we were done." It seemed like something awfully innocuous to find out something so momentous.

"They'll know tomorrow?"

"That's what the nurse said." Piper had tried to dissuade Zephyr from coming to the doctor's office with her.

It wasn't as if she was having a difficult procedure, or something. But he'd insisted and now, she was kind of glad.

He put his hand out to take hers and led her outside. It was one of Seattle's rare sunny days. Not so uncommon in the summer, but not something to be taken for granted, either.

"I'm glad I'm not alone, which makes me feel like a real wuss," she admitted.

"You are facing the possibility of a major life change. That cannot help but be disconcerting. You are no weakling."

She smiled up at him and squeezed his hand. "Well, I'm glad you're here." Even if she hadn't wanted it that way at first.

"I am glad to be here."

"Do you have to go into the office today?" she asked as they settled into his Mercedes.

"No, but I did promise to have dinner with Cass and Neo tonight."

"Oh, okay." She pasted a bright smile on her face. "If you

could just drop me at my apartment. I'll drive to the office from there."

Or close her shades, put in the Coco Chanel biography she'd been meaning to watch and eat that pint of triple chocolate decadence hiding in the back corner of her freezer. It wasn't as if she had to go to work. She was her own boss. If she wanted a day off to wallow in worry, she could take it.

"Dinner isn't until this evening, and I was hoping you would come with me."

"Oh."

"I have no intention of leaving you alone to dwell."

He knew her too well. "Who said anything about dwelling?"

"We have been friends for years."

"Are you implying that makes you a mind reader?"

"I only wish—" he smiled "—but I do know you."

"Yes, you do."

"So, dinner with Cass and Neo?"

"Sure." She bit her lip and looked out the window. "You know Cass and I have never actually met."

"I know. It is time."

"Because I might be pregnant."

"Because you are my close friend and so are they," he explained.

"So we should all know each other?"

"Naturally."

"Your arrogance is showing again," she teased.

"But remember, you find it charming."

"It's a good thing for you that I do."

"Do you need to work today?" he asked this time.

"I have a few small jobs I could work on finishing up before your project swallows all my time." But she really didn't want to deal with any of them.

"Is that what you want to do?"

"No."

"Well, then?"

"There's a pint of chocolate ice cream in my freezer with my name on it." Piper clung on to her original plans.

"Really? I was unaware your name was triple chocolate decadence."

"You've been snooping in my cold storage?" She tried to sound outraged, but only managed mildly amused.

"Business tycoons crave ice cream, too. Even Greek ones."

"You ate my triple chocolate decadence?" The outrage came through bright and clear this time.

"Of course not. I ate the single-serving cherries jubilee buried behind the vegetarian meals you never eat but buy to make yourself feel better about your food purchasing habits."

She ignored the jab about her sadly ignored healthier food options. "I like cherries jubilee."

"With a healthy dose of hot fudge perhaps."

"Okay, so, I'm a chocoholic. Is that a crime?"

"Not in Seattle, home to more chocolate-flavored coffees than most small countries." He sounded indulgent. She loved him in this mood.

"Oooh, an iced mocha latte sounds good." Could she have caffeine if she was pregnant? "Maybe decaffeinated."

"We'll go through a coffee-shop drive thru."

"Why not stop somewhere?" she asked.

"Because I indulged your museum obsession in Athens, today is your day to indulge mine."

"You want to go to museums?"

"I have other obsessions," he said as he pulled up next to a coffee shack.

"You do? Other than making money, I wasn't aware."

"Right. You are probably the only person in the world besides Neo that knows that for the lie it is." They both made their orders and then he gave her a significant look. "You are one of those obsessions."

"You're turning into quite the silver-tongued devil, you know that?"

"I have always been good with my mouth."

"That can certainly be taken more than one way."

"You should know."

She felt herself blushing, despite their history together. Nevertheless, she agreed. "I do."

The young barista cleared his throat. With a blush darker than hers burning on his cheeks, he handed Zephyr their drinks.

Zephyr pulled his car back out onto the road. "You are not my only interest, however."

"My feelings might be hurt if you hadn't downgraded whatever you're going to try to talk me into from an obsession, which I am, to an *interest*."

"I like fish."

"I had noticed." Her blue eyes queried where he was going with this. "You eat it more often than either steak or chicken."

"Not to eat. To watch."

"You want to go whale watching?" she guessed.

"Not today. I was thinking the aquarium." That was so not what she expected to hear.

"You want to go the Seattle Aquarium…but that's for children."

"*I* don't think so."

"Seriously…you've been?"

"Several times."

Wow…just wow. "No way."

"I go when I need a place to think. Watching the fish can be very soothing."

"Even with all those children around?"

"I like to see happy families."

Somewhere over the Atlantic, Zephyr had become convinced that Piper was indeed pregnant. Regardless of the statistical probability after her years on the birth control patch. Therefore, he needed to convince her that marriage to him was a good option for her future, even without the love.

He wouldn't give her love, but he realized he could give her more of himself. It went against his desire for self-protection, but he now considered his sharing of his past with her as a brilliant tactical move on his part. Piper needed to feel emotionally connected to people she cared about. He had seen the effect his sharing had had on her.

She'd drawn closer to him even as he'd attempted to back-track to a shallower level of emotional intimacy. With his baby's future on the line, he could and would give Piper a stronger connection, despite the fact he had no intention of allowing himself to be vulnerable to romantic love, were he even capable of the emotion.

Going to the aquarium wasn't some big romantic thing, but it would allow Piper to glimpse a part of his life he did not share with others. It wasn't much, but his instincts told him that sharing this habit with her would work toward convincing her they could have a strong enough marriage to raise children in.

Piper enjoyed the aquarium more than she thought she would. A lot more, but what she found most intriguing was watching the way Zephyr watched the other people there. She was sure he had no idea just how much his expression revealed of the inner man. His mouth would tilt in a half smile every time a child made an enthusiastic noise to its mother or father.

He watched the antics of the little ones with an indulgent grin and looked with pure longing at more than one set of parents visiting the aquarium with their kids.

"You really enjoy being here, don't you?" she asked him in the glassed-in tunnel of exotic fish.

"Very much." He looked around them with a wistful expression that was there and gone in a blink. "Everyone here has normal lives."

"You assume."

"I assume." He smiled ruefully at her correction.

"You have a normal life. Now."

"Do I?"

"Yes, of course," she said.

"I'm a workaholic tycoon that spends most of his time making money and creating places for other people to enjoy the fruits of theirs."

"So, spend some time enjoying them yourself."

"Alone?"

"You aren't alone right now." If she didn't know better, she would think he was making his case for how much he needed his own family.

"No, I am not."

"Does that make you happy?" she couldn't help asking.

"Yes, I like being here, in one of my favorite places, *with you*."

"It's special." Really, really special. And he was sharing it with her. She reached up and kissed the corner of his mouth. "Thank you."

They both stepped to the side as a young boy went racing by, his older brother right behind him and a woman even farther back calling for them to slow down.

Looking harried, but smiling, she rushed to catch up. "Sorry about that. They're both crazy for the otter exhibit."

Zephyr tilted his head. "No problem. You're lucky to have such active children."

"That's one way to look at it." But her grin as she sprinted after her children said she saw it the same.

"You really do want children, for more than just having someone to pass on your legacy of wealth." How could she have thought anything else?

He looked down at her, his dark eyes filled with a longing she was just beginning to understand ran soul deep for him. "Yes."

Lost to anyone else around them, she reached up to cup his cheek. "You'll make a wonderful father."

"That is my sincere hope."

* * *

Cass was wearing a beautiful bright dress when she opened Neo's apartment door to Zephyr and Piper later that evening.

She grinned at Zephyr and pulled him in for a hug. "Long time, no see, stranger. How was Greece?"

"Warm and beautiful."

"You mean you actually took time to notice. When Neo told me you were taking a minivacation before going to the island, I almost fainted, but I'm glad."

"Hey, I am not as bad as my business partner."

"Only a robot works as many hours and holidays as Neo did before we met, but he's well on his way to reformed now."

The complacency in Cass's voice made him smile. "I noticed."

Cass turned to Piper. "Please tell me you're taking on the job for Zee. He needs someone to."

"Don't answer that," Zephyr demanded, then said, "*Yineka mou*, this is my best friend's fiancée, Cassandra Baker, world-renowned pianist and composer. Cass, this is Piper Madison, brilliant designer and my very good friend."

Cass's brows rose to her hairline and Zephyr realized he had made a mistake using that particular endearment in front of her. No doubt Neo had long since told her the translation and the implications often associated with it. Implications he was becoming more and more comfortable with.

Cass took both of Piper's hands in hers and squeezed them. "So, it *is* your job."

"I'm beginning to think so, yes." Piper glanced at him out of the corner of her eye. "Good friends have an obligation to look out for each other."

"That's the argument Zee used when talking me into taking the piano lessons that changed my life," Neo said as he came into the entryway. "Shouldn't we all go into the living room? It's got more comfortable seating."

He gave Piper a smile that seemed to startle her, but she

returned the gesture and said, "Good to see you again, Neo."

Then Cass led Piper away by the hand while Neo hung back to give Zephyr a traditional Greek greeting. "It is good to have you back in Seattle."

"I miss the island already."

"I felt the same after leaving." Neo nodded. "It is a special place."

"Special enough to consider making it a more regular aspect of my life."

"You are serious?"

"What would you think of delegating another level of responsibility to our well-trained staff and moving our offices to the island villa?"

Neo's eyes widened in shock. "You *are* serious."

"Never more so."

"Something has happened."

Zephyr shrugged, but was feeling nothing like complacent. "I'm ready to make changes in my life."

"Do you have news to share with me?"

"Not yet."

"But there will be?" Neo pressed.

"Perhaps."

"You're going to have to do better than that."

Not yet. "Give me until tomorrow."

Neo didn't push. Cass would have. Zephyr could just be thankful his friend would not have a chance to bring it up to her while Zephyr and Piper were there.

They walked into the living room to find Cass and Piper ensconced on the sofa going through digital pictures of the trip to Greece on Piper's minitablet PC.

"I didn't realize you'd brought that," Zephyr said as he took the chair next to Piper's spot on the sofa.

Neo sat beside his fiancée.

"I thought they might be interested in your trip."

"Our trip."

She rolled her eyes. "Our trip."

"I'd really like to go to this art museum while we're there," Cass said to Neo.

He kissed her temple. "Then we will definitely add that to our agenda."

"You're going to Greece soon?" Piper asked.

Cass beamed. "For our honeymoon."

"I seem to remember reading that you'd been there in a tour when you were younger."

"Yes." Cass looked a little startled. "You read about me?"

Piper blushed, but smiled. "When Zephyr told me Neo was getting married, I was understandably curious about the woman who had managed to lead him to such a human endeavor."

Cass laughed out loud. "Wow, and you told me once that Zephyr was the only person that really knew you well."

"I've worked for Stamos and Nikos Enterprises a few times." Piper gave them a look rife with meaning. "I met Neo on a couple of the projects, though he wasn't coordinating them."

"And you found me inhuman?" Neo asked, contriving to sound offended.

"You were so intimidating that I sent up a prayer of thanks you were not the lead on the project I'd been hired for." She winked conspiratorially at Cass. "I thought Zephyr was so much more laid-back and would be a much easier man to work for."

"But you learned the truth?" Cass asked with a teasing glance to Zephyr.

"It took a bit, but I did."

Zephyr feigned shock. "So, you *don't* think I'm easy to work for?"

"I think anyone excellent at their job, who makes a minimum of mistakes, if none at all, and who understands how very seriously you take the success of each development, will find you a pussycat to work for."

"That's a lot of caveats," Neo said, laughing.

Cass raised her brows at her fiancé. "I thought she did an admirable job of being diplomatic."

"I'm not sure if that was a character assassination, or an endorsement," Zephyr admitted.

"See? Diplomatic," Cass teased.

"Zephyr, you are an amazing man, but just like Neo, you're just a little superhuman for the rest of us. You just hide your intensity behind your charm."

"Are you saying I am not charming?" Neo demanded.

Piper made a zipping motion over her sealed lips and they all burst out laughing.

Cass leaned against Neo and rubbed her head against his shoulder. "Don't worry, Superman, I like you just the way you are."

Seeing his friends like this usually gave Zephyr a twinge of useless envy, but tonight all he felt was a fleeting hope Piper was seeing it, too. And perhaps realizing a reformed Greek street kid wasn't such a bad horse to place her wager on.

"Arrogance and all?" Neo prompted Cass.

She smiled and patted his leg. "That's part of your charm."

Neo gave Piper a triumphant look. "See, I *do* have charm."

"I can attest to the arrogance part of it, anyway," Piper said with a cheeky grin. "You and Zephyr both have bigger than the average dose."

"Has he not told you that if it is justified, then we are talking about confidence here?" Neo asked.

"That's right," Zephyr agreed.

Both Cass and Piper simply laughed and shook their heads.

"Want to see the pictures?" Piper asked Neo.

"But of course. I would like evidence of Zee playing the tourist."

"Well, here he is haggling with the jeweler in the Plaka over a necklace." She clicked to one of the photos he had not known Piper had taken. It showed him in animated conversation with a short, square Greek about twenty years Zephyr's senior.

"I thought you weren't supposed to try to bargain inside actual shops," Cass asked. "I've been reading up on it."

Zephyr waved his hand in dismissal. A Greek boy who made his livelihood on the streets of Athens learned to bargain with the taxman, if that's what it took. "What could it hurt to try? I was buying an expensive piece. If he wanted to move it that day, he needed to offer me an incentive."

"And did he?" Cass asked.

Piper laughed out loud at that. "Do you really need to ask? Of course. No one in their right mind says no to billionaire tycoon Zephyr Nikos."

"Remember that tomorrow," Zephyr said under his breath.

But they all three heard him and gave him looks of inquiry in varying degrees.

He shrugged. "Show Cass the pictures of the view of Athens from the Acropolis."

"Never mind that," Cass said. "Do you know what he's talking about, Piper?"

Piper frowned at him. "I do and it's not something I'm comfortable discussing right now."

"Does it have anything to do with why Zephyr asked me about moving the head offices to the island villa?" Neo asked.

Zephyr winced and bit back a particularly virulent curse.

"You did what?" Piper demanded, shock blatant in every centimeter of her lovely face.

"What?" screeched Cass. She gave Neo a confused look. "You told me we had to wait to talk to him about it until we'd been married at least a year!"

"You and Cass have already discussed it?" Zephyr asked, taking his turn at being taken aback.

"We've discussed many options for the future. Cassandra wants to experience other parts of the world and I want her to have every opportunity for maximum happiness," Neo said with a shrug.

Now, *that* did not surprise him. With more trepidation than he had felt since leaving Greece for the unknown, Zephyr shifted his gaze to Piper to see how she was taking this discussion.

Her azure eyes were fixed on him with steady intensity. "You're going to pull out all the stops if that test comes back positive, aren't you?"

"Would you expect anything different?" He was ruthless, but not dishonest.

"I guess not. I was trying very hard not to think about it at all, though." Her voice was tinged with rueful inevitability.

He did not know if that was good, or bad. "I am sorry."

"For showing your hand early?"

"For making you think about it."

"What exactly is it we're thinking about?" Neo asked in a voice others had learned not to ignore.

Luckily for Zephyr, he wasn't other people and he had no trouble ignoring his best friend and business partner's demand.

Piper closed her eyes with every evidence of counting to ten and he thought she'd probably succeed in ignoring Neo, too.

But then Cass elbowed her nosy fiancé. "Leave them alone, Neo." Then she sighed. "Besides, it's obvious and not something Piper should be forced to discuss before she's certain one way, or the other."

"One way, or the other, what?" Neo actually sounded plaintive.

Zephyr could not remember the last time he had heard that particular tone from Neo, but it had been at least a decade, probably longer. He had no idea how Piper would react to it. He thanked God and the angels besides when she laughed.

"So, what's for dinner?" she asked.

Even Neo knew enough to allow the subject change to pass without incident.

The rest of the evening went well, considering. Cass kept Neo in line and Piper did her best to ignore any and all leading comments and questions.

But she didn't turn toward his door when they left Neo's penthouse. Instead, she headed for the elevator.

He put his hand on her shoulder as she pressed the button. "Where are you going?"

"Home." She sighed and looked back at him. "I need some time to myself, Zephyr."

Unexpectedly, the request hit him in that place permanently wounded when his mother left him in the orphanage and never took him home with her again.

Even so, he asked, "Are you sure? You seem to sleep well in my arms."

"I'm not sure I'm going to sleep at all." Unfortunately, she looked like the thing she needed most right then was a good night's rest.

In his bed, snuggled against him, damn it.

But clearly, she did not agree. She did not want or need him right then. Maybe not at all.

"An even better reason for you not to be alone."

She shook her head, a sad look passing over her face. "I'm sorry."

Pleading not to be left behind when someone was intent on leaving you did no good. That was a lesson he had learned even better than how to make money and at a much younger age. But it still took an inordinate amount of inner fortitude to drop his hand from her shoulder.

He stepped back. "You will call me when you get word?" He did not like asking. It reminded him of asking for his mother's consideration and getting excuses for why things could not be different.

"Yes, of course."

But she did not.

Zephyr forced himself to wait until after lunch to try calling her. Surely, the doctor would have contacted her by now. His call went straight to voice mail, though. He did not bother to leave a message.

An hour later, he called her home, but got her voice mail again. At the office, her assistant answered the phone. However, she informed him that Piper was not in and not expected today.

Neo walked into Zephyr's office later that afternoon, after Zephyr had called Piper yet again, only to get the too professional message on her voice mail box.

"You look like hell. What's going on?" Neo demanded.

Without having to consider it, Zephyr told him. Everything.

"You should have brought her to meet Cassandra and I before last night," was Neo's first reaction.

"Why?" Neo had never been particularly interested in socializing with Zephyr's other friends, unless it advanced their company's interest.

"You have been in a sexual relationship with Piper for months and friends for over two years. How did I not know this?" Neo asked, rather than answering.

"You knew we were friends."

"Not that good of friends." Neo shook his head. "She's the reason you told me sex with a friend was so good, isn't she?"

"Yes."

"Have you been with anyone else sexually since you began your relationship with Piper?"

"Do you really think that is any of your business?"

"Probably not, but answer anyway," Neo insisted.

"Once, before I realized the first time wasn't going to be a single shot."

"And that did not tell you anything?"

"What? I like intimacy with Piper. I am too busy with our company to expend energy on other women."

Neo's lips twisted in a mocking frown. "How long has your head been in the dark place?"

Zephyr remembered accusing Neo of having his head up

his ass once, in regard to Cass. Apparently this was pay-back. "It's not. We both knew what we had and what we did not have."

"And now?"

"And now she may be pregnant with my child."

"So, that changes everything?" Neo asked.

"Naturally."

"Why?"

"You can ask?" After the way they had both grown up, he would expect Neo to be the first to understand.

"You are not taking my point," Neo said with exasperation. "Don't you see that she is bound to think you are only wanting marriage because of the baby?"

"That *is* the only reason. I would not have considered it otherwise."

"Why the hell not?"

"She deserves better."

For the second time in less than twenty-four hours, Neo looked absolutely gobsmacked. "You *are* the best."

"You are prejudiced." But the belligerent certainty in his friend's voice was surprisingly nice to hear.

"I am your brother, Cass says so. That means I'm allowed."

Zephyr felt warmth he hadn't known in decades, but he didn't let it show on his face. He was no pushover despite these weird emotional twinges he was experiencing. "So, step outside your personal bias and look at this from Piper's perspective."

"I do not see the distinction here." Neo's eyes filled with something far too close to pity for Zephyr's comfort. "You're a good man, Zephyr."

"I did not say I wasn't." Merely that Piper deserved better than what he had to offer her.

"So, what is the problem?"

"She wants to be *in love* with her next husband," Zephyr explained grimly. "Like she was with Art."

"And you do not love her?"

"No."

"Bull."

Zephyr shook his head. "Love doesn't work for everybody." At least on that truth, he was one hundred percent convinced. And he was one of those people.

Neo sighed. "You're right, but giving up before you even try isn't like you."

"Sometimes trying is the stupidest thing of all to do."

"That does not sound like you."

"And you sound like a broken record," Zephyr retorted.

"So, say something that makes me understand this defeatist attitude of yours."

"She left last night."

"When you wanted her to stay." Neo knew him so well, he did not even have to make it a question.

"She said she was sorry." Just like his mother had done, over and over again—first when leaving him behind and then when she refused to bring his little sister back to visit.

In situations like this, sorry didn't mean anything.

"She also said she would call you, *ne*?"

"Yes."

"So, trust her to do it."

"When?" Zephyr snapped.

"When she is ready."

"You were not this complacent with Cass."

"I was in love with Cassandra." Neo's look challenged Zephyr.

Apparently, if he was not in love, he had no right to be worried, cautious or impatient. Like hell. "So, because I'm not playing the romantic hero, I have to wait and wonder if my lover carries my child?"

"You have to wait because she will call when she is ready and not before."

"I am well aware of that." And it was doing nothing for his mood, which he was sure was obvious, even to Neo.

Neo looked at him like he was a newly discovered species. "I still cannot believe you had a lover for almost a year and I did not know it."

"I did not consider her my lover."

An unholy light gleamed in Neo's eyes. "My friend, this just gets better and better. When did *that* change?"

"In Greece."

"That trip had a pretty big impact even before the missing birth control patch was discovered."

"If you say so."

"What I say does not matter. On the other hand, what you and Piper say is of utmost importance."

"She *said* she would call, and she has not," Zephyr all but growled.

"Be patient and believe in your friendship if you will believe in nothing else."

"I have no other option."

"Then make it work for you, that is what men like us do. We do not give up."

That was one truth Zephyr could not deny.

Neo left and Zephyr forced himself to get to work on the piles of urgent papers and messages stacked on top of his desk from his time out of the office. It was nine o'clock that night before he admitted temporary defeat and left his office.

Piper still had not called, though he had called her on the hour, every hour, since the afternoon.

Piper sat outside the Seattle Aquarium, watching children and adults come and go. Her hand rested against her lower abdomen. She didn't feel any different. Her body had not changed at all, but inside her womb a baby grew. Her baby. Zephyr's baby. Their child.

The wholly unexpected fulfillment of one of her dearest hopes.

She should have called right away and told him the news,

but she couldn't. She had to think and she couldn't do that around him right now.

She loved a man who had taken great pains to make sure she understood he would never love her. And that same man was going to ask her to marry him. She was sure of it.

Because she carried his child.

In a normal world, that would result in an immediate and outright refusal on her part. Before meeting and falling in love with Zephyr Nikos, she would never have even considered for one second marrying a man who did not profess to love her. But Zephyr's perspective was a unique one.

In his world, love guaranteed nothing but pain. He hadn't come out and said so, but his story about his past made that clear. He had loved his mother and she had abandoned him to an orphanage. He had loved both of his half siblings, but they had been taken from him.

Even if he did love Piper, he might never be able to admit it.

One of the questions that chased round and round in her brain was whether or not she could accept that and marry him anyway. She had no doubts about her ability to raise this child on her own. She was an educated woman with her own successful business. She wasn't a billionaire, but she wasn't a pauper, either.

Zephyr could be part of the baby's life without marrying her as well. But he couldn't be a full-time dad if they didn't live together. Even in the best shared custody arrangements, both parents were forced to take a less pervasive role in their child's life.

And Zephyr wasn't going to be content with the role of part-time dad. Just because she refused to marry him did not mean he would not one day marry. He didn't just want to be a father; he wanted a family. That had been obvious when they'd visited the aquarium together.

He wanted what he saw all around him, and she could not blame him.

Which led to the other question that chased the first one over and over again: could she bear to stand aside while he married another woman and built a whole family with her? Could she stand her own child only having half-time with his or her daddy while others that came later got him each and every day?

Unlike Zephyr, her time at the Seattle Aquarium was doing nothing to help her think of answers to those hard questions.

Zephyr let himself into his empty apartment, annoyed when he realized the cleaning service had left the lights on in the living room again. His power bill was not the issue; indiscriminate wasteful use of the planet's resources was.

It had been almost a week since Piper was supposed to have called him. She hadn't been in to work, at least according to her assistant, Brandi. He'd gone by Piper's apartment, but she hadn't answered the door. Her phone had to be off and he'd finally stopped calling, but each day that went by echoed feelings he thought he would never again have to experience.

The fear of being abandoned was a live thing inside of him, but he hid it, even from Neo. He couldn't stand the feeling of helplessness that grew with every hour she did not call. Had he lost his friend? Was she going to try to keep him from his child if she was indeed pregnant?

One thing he knew was that he might feel helpless, but he wasn't. If she carried his child, she was not going to keep it away from him like his brother and sister had been. He would be a part of this child's life, even if marrying its mother wasn't an option.

He would fight for custody. She could be the weekend parent, if she didn't want to marry him. She was still building her business, she'd said so herself. He could free more of his time to parent their child hands-on and any decent judge would see that.

Disgusted with the direction of his thoughts, he yanked off his already loosened tie as he strode into the living room. He stopped dead at the sight that greeted him.

Piper was curled on his sofa, under a quilt he had brought back from Greece many years ago. As if she could sense his presence, her eyelids fluttered and then opened.

She gazed up at him drowsily. "Hi."

"You said you would call."

"I couldn't. I had to think."

"So, you left me hanging for almost a week?"

She flinched at the ice in his voice, but he could not help that. "I decided it wasn't something we should discuss on the phone but, um…maybe I should have called and told you that."

"Yes, you should have. I have been worried. I went by your apartment. You did not answer the door."

"I wasn't there. I went to *my* favorite place to think after trying yours and getting nowhere."

"Where is that?" he demanded.

"The beach."

"You could not have let me know you went out of town?"

"If I had called you, you would have talked me into seeing you."

"Maybe because that was what we both needed." Frustrated anger laced his voice. "At the very least, you could have let me know that you were waiting here today."

"I should have," she acknowledged as she sat up and brushed her hair back off her face. The beach might be her favorite place to think, but it had brought her no peace and despite just waking from a nap, she looked like she hadn't been getting enough sleep. "I was just so tired and thought you would come up after work. I didn't realize you would work until bedtime."

"It is hardly that."

"Close enough."

"Damn it! Do not try to sidestep the issue. If I had known you were here, I would have left my office immediately." He took a deep breath and let it out slowly to prevent his volume from increasing. "I was worried. Do you understand that?" Did she care? "I called your cell over and over again."

She looked down so he could not see her eyes, and target the guilt he would see there. "I turned it off."

"I figured that out."

She nodded. She stood up and came to him, then tilted her head back so their gazes met. Emotions he did not understand swirled in her blue depths.

"Tell me," he demanded, his tone softer than he intended. How could he help feeling compassion? She looked like hell.

"I'm sorry I didn't call. It was inconsiderate and selfish of me. I should have called, no matter how hard it would have been. I kept thinking and thinking, but I couldn't make sense of anything no matter which way I looked at it. When I finally got here today, it was past four. I really thought I'd take a short nap and you would be here. And then we could talk."

"Instead I worked late, trying to keep my mind off the fact you did not keep your promise to call." Almost a week ago, but he had already said that and she had acknowledged it.

She nodded. "This situation is scary, Zephyr."

"I agree, but I would think that two friends facing down fear together would work better than each trying deal with it on his or her own."

"I'm sure you're right." She looked away again. "I just…I knew you'd want to get married and I didn't know what I wanted to do about that."

"So, you *are* pregnant."

She met his gaze, hers suspiciously glossy. "Yes, we're either very unlucky or wildly fortunate, depending on how you want to look at it."

"How do *you* look at it?" he demanded.

"Wildly fortunate? How else? I'm thrilled to be having your baby even if this whole situation scares me to death." She looked ready to shake apart.

Damn it. He would have noticed how fragile she was earlier if he hadn't been working through his own turmoil. He did not want to tell her the plans he'd been making when he first arrived, but would she give him a choice?

Hoping to convince her of their best option yet, he pulled her into his arms, keeping their gazes connected even as their bodies pressed together in comfort. "What are you so frightened of?"

"A lot of things."

"What scares you the most?"

"That I'll agree to marry you, we'll do the deed and then you'll finally fall in love—*with someone else*."

That was at the top of her fear factor list? He couldn't have been more stunned if she said she was terrified of an alien invasion snatching their baby from her womb. "I am not going to fall in love with another woman."

"You can't be sure of that."

"Yes, I can. Trust me, Piper. It is not even a possibility." Of all the things he'd been considering over her week-long silence, that was not one of them.

"Do you think there is even a tiny chance that someday you might fall in love with me?" She buried her face against his chest and waited for his answer.

He wanted to lie; it would make things so much easier, but he could not. "If I was capable of falling in love, I already would have."

"You really believe that?"

"Absolutely."

Her head tilted back so he could see her glare. "Everyone is capable of love."

"That is debatable."

"Yes, I guess it is." She grimaced. "There are certainly people that make a great case for that point of view anyway. I never considered you one of them, however."

He could not help that. He shrugged. "What else scares you?"

"Oh, the usual, what will happen to my business, what if I lose the baby, what if I'm a terrible mother, am I going to turn into a whale, can I learn Greek?" Her litany of worries came out in a voice garbled by suppressed tears he did not know what to do about.

"You are going to marry me." Why else would she need to learn Greek?

"How can I do anything else? I've looked at this situation from every side until I'm sick with it. If I don't marry you, we'll have to share custody and I'm not naive enough to think you are going to settle for being a weekend dad. You'll fight for at least equal custody, if not majority custody."

He was shocked. She realized that. "I…"

"Don't try to deny it."

"I wasn't going to."

Her lips trembled, but she blinked away the incipient moisture in her troubled blue eyes. "Good. We can't build a marriage on lies."

"I agree."

"The custody issue wasn't even the most distressing."

"It was not?" What could have worried her more?

"No. It was the certainty that if I didn't marry you, one day you would marry someone else and build a whole family with them."

"The thought of me married to someone else bothers you?" he asked, just to clarify. She had left him without any sort of contact for almost a week after all.

"Of course it does. *I love you.*"

Something inside his chest stuttered. "You love me?"

"Yes."

"Like a friend." He attempted to qualify.

She wrapped her arms around his neck and shook her head, those terrifying tears of hers spilling over now. "No, not like a friend."

"You won't convince anyone you love me like a brother." Maybe there was some special kind of love women left for the father of their children.

She shook her head again, a mysterious smile flirting with

the edge of her lips, despite the sadness in her eyes. "Like the only man in my universe, like the other half of my heart, like the part of my soul that's been missing my whole life but I didn't know it."

He would have staggered if they hadn't been holding each other so tightly. "Is that how you loved Art?" He did not know why he asked except for as some form of penance, because one thing he *never* wanted to hear was that she had loved her ex like that.

"My feelings for Art weren't even a shadow of what is in my heart for you."

Could he believe that? And if he did, what difference did it make? His mother had loved him, too, but she'd walked away when a choice had to be made. "And yet, you did not call."

"Loving you doesn't make me perfect, or even perfectly unselfish. In fact, it makes me terribly self-focused because it makes me so vulnerable to being hurt by you. I *want* to marry you so I know you won't—*can't*—leave me." The tears were in her voice now. "I want to be with you for the rest of my life and I wanted to be pregnant so bad, it was an ache in my gut that wouldn't let me sleep at all the night before the doctor's office called. I spent the darkest hours of that night in a perfect agony of guilt and unable to change my desires one jot even because of it. Did you hear all those *I*'s and *me*'s?"

"You *wanted* to carry my child?" he asked, ignoring self-flagellating guilt.

"Yes, more than anything. Which probably makes you wonder if I lost my patch on purpose, but I swear to you that I didn't."

"Of course not, but why did you want to?"

"Have you been listening to me at all? I knew a baby would tie you to me. Not because I'm not capable of being a single mother, but because you would not want me to be. I'm really ashamed of feeling that way, but I can't change it. I never would have done it on purpose, but I won't pretend I don't feel *wildly fortunate*, either. Which probably should make *you* reconsider whether or not you should marry me."

"So, if you wanted it so bad, why stay away so long?"

"Because when I got what I thought I wanted, I pictured a lifetime of being married to a man who is not in love with me and it terrified me."

"You have been so unhappy these past months?"

"No."

"Then, why should you be unhappy as my wife?" he demanded. Didn't she see how illogical she was being?

"I'm hoping I won't be."

"I'll make sure of it." She was going to accuse him of arrogance again, but before she got a chance, he decided to offer his own truth. "I also wanted you to be pregnant and I am very glad you have decided to marry me."

He could not resist the expression his words brought to her face, he kissed her and they spent several minutes lost in a very pleasant joint effort to leave an indelible mark on the other's lips.

"Do you think our mutual selfishness negates itself?" she asked as if the answer really mattered to her.

"I think that as long as we are both pleased with the outcome, it does not matter."

"I think maybe you're right." She looked up at him through her lashes. "Can we make love now?"

"Is it safe for the baby?"

"Very."

"You asked?"

"Of course I did. I know what we're like together and we are going to be together a lot now."

He liked the sound of that, though a tiny voice inside warned him not to get too used to it as it could all be taken away. After all, she had cut herself off from him while making her decision, showing she did not *need* him even if she loved him. "You'll move in with me?"

"This weekend."

"We are not sleeping apart again meantime."

"No, but I need to work and won't have time to pack for the move until the weekend."

"I'll hire movers."

"I'll still need to be there to supervise."

He could not argue that. "Do you want a big wedding?"

"No." She gave him a nervous look complete with a bitten bottom lip. "I just want our families there."

"I don't have any family."

"Oh, yes you do. I know your secrets now. Besides Neo, who is your brother in everything but genetics, there is your mother, her husband and your half siblings, et al. And I want them at our wedding."

"Why?"

"Because someday, I think it's going to matter to you that they were there. Besides, it will hurt your sister's feelings if we don't invite her."

"Why do you think so?" Piper saw things so differently than he did; he didn't always understand what made her say the things she did.

"She insisted on you meeting her children, didn't she? She considers you her brother and she'd be devastated if she discovered you didn't feel the same."

"I do. For good, or ill, she is my sister."

"It's all to the good."

"So you say."

"I'm almost a mother. I'm practically an oracle now. It comes with the territory," she said, tongue firmly in cheek.

And he laughed like he was supposed to before sweeping her into his arms. Making love sounded better than talking about his family. "What you are now, is mine."

"You seem pretty pleased about that." She didn't sound too disappointed by the prospect herself.

"I am." He carried her down the hall to his...to *their* bedroom.

"Are we really moving to Greece?" she asked between baby kisses smattered along his jaw.

"The island would be a good place to raise children."

"Yes, but I'd marry you regardless."

"You said you wanted it."

"I do." She grabbed his face, making him look her in the eye. "This isn't a business transaction. I don't love your money, or what it can buy for me. I love you, Zephyr."

She said so, but she'd still left him and not called for almost a week. Maybe Zephyr did not understand love, but he did not think it should be so easy to hurt someone if you loved them. He wasn't about to dwell on that now though, no more than he'd spent time pining over his mother's defection once he'd learned he had to accept it. Piper had agreed to marry him, even though, technically, he had not asked.

That was all that mattered right now.

Without answering her assertion, Zephyr carried Piper into the bedroom and laid her on the bed oh, so carefully. She smiled up at him, but he put his finger up with the gesture to wait a minute.

He leaned over and grabbed the phone from beside the bed, then pressed two buttons.

"Memory" and "One" she would bet.

Someone picked up on the other end.

"Congratulate me. We are going to have a baby and Piper has agreed to marry me." He smiled down at her while speaking into the phone.

Excited words in a definite masculine tone came through the headset, though they were too muffled to understand.

"Yes. I'll call you with details tomorrow."

Neo said something else.

"I will," Zephyr replied. *"Kalinichta."*

He hung up the phone.

"Neo?" she asked, just to be sure.

"Yes. He knew I was waiting for your phone call. He was concerned about me." And even on the verge of making love to her, Zephyr thought to call his friend and settle his mind.

Maybe he'd wanted to share his news, too.

"You're a special man, Zephyr Nikos. Is he happy for you?"

"For us both. He and Cass will take us out tomorrow to celebrate if you are willing."

"Of course. Though I'll have to work during the day. I've taken way more time off than I should have."

"Do you think Brandi will relocate to the island with Cerulean Designs?"

"I'd like to ask her, but I don't know if I can continue to pay her salary once I cut back on my client list." Piper decided to begin undressing and remind Zephyr why he'd carried her in here to begin with. "I don't want to work anywhere near full-time if I don't have to."

Chocolate-dark eyes ate her alive as she peeled off her comfort jeans and T-shirt. "I am very pleased to hear that. We will work something out regarding Brandi."

"You mean you're going to offer to pay her." She paused in the act of unhooking her bra.

He could try to deny it, but she knew him. And his expression said he was already busy trying to come up with a compelling reason for doing so, given enough time.

"Why did you name your company Cerulean Designs?" he asked in an obvious bid to change the subject.

"Nice feint, but don't think I've forgotten this discussion."

"You haven't forgotten we were about to make love, either, have you?"

"I'm not the one still completely dressed."

"I can fix that quickly enough."

CHAPTER SEVEN

"Do IT."

Zephyr kicked off his designer loafers with two audible thumps as they landed somewhere on the carpet.

"After everything went down with my ex, I didn't have a lot to smile about, much less laugh," Piper said, answering his previous question. "I was watching a gay romance movie when the guy planning the wedding started yelling at his fabric supplier. The wedding planner was incensed that the supplier didn't know what cerulean was, much less how to spell it. I realized I didn't know what cerulean was, either, and I was an interior designer. I learned later it was the same shade of blue as my eyes, which I thought was sort of prophetic. Anyway, I started laughing at the movie, really amused, for the first time in too long. I named my company Cerulean Designs to remind myself that no matter what was going on in my life, there was always a reason to laugh."

Zephyr stopped undressing and stared down at her. "That's a great story."

"It's a good memory. It doesn't hurt to have the everyday reminder that I don't know all there is to know about design, either."

"Keeping you humble and positive at the same time. That's a lot of mileage for one business name." He pulled off his unbuttoned shirt and suit jacket in one go.

"Your turn."

"I'm already undressing."

"I mean to answer a question."

"Oh, okay. What?"

"Why Stamos and Nikos Enterprises as opposed to the other way around?"

"It was nothing so meaning-driven," he said as he pushed his slacks and boxers down his legs with impatient speed.

"What was it?"

"We flipped a coin for it. Neo won the toss."

She was still laughing when he came down over her completely, deliciously, wonderfully naked, and kissed the joy right from her lips. It tasted good, better than good—it was perfect.

"So, it doesn't bother you that we're getting married so close to you and Neo?" Piper asked Cass the next day when the other woman called to congratulate her.

"Not at all. I think it's fantastic you two want to get married in Greece. As you know, we're going to be there on our honeymoon, anyway."

"Zephyr's flying my parents and sibs to Athens for the ceremony." She'd been happy when they had all promised to attend. Of course, a paid-for vacation to Greece was nothing to sneeze at. And didn't that make her sound as cynical about money as her groom-to-be?

"Neo said Zephyr's inviting his own family," Cass said, unaware of Piper's cynical thoughts. "Neither of us even knew he was still in touch with them."

"His relationship with his mom is pretty complicated." Zephyr had taken Neo out to lunch and told his best friend the truth of his past, so Piper didn't have to sidestep the issue, but she didn't want to get into it too deeply, either.

Cass whistled softly. "You can say that again. I'm not sure, but I think Neo might have been better off losing his mom to an overdose than to a better life. That had to do a real number of Zephyr's ability to trust."

To love, as well, but Piper wasn't getting into that. "Between our two families, there will be less than two dozen guests. You'll be okay with that, won't you?"

"I am." The satisfaction and shy pride in Cass's voice was a truly lovely sound. "My agoraphobia is so much better now. I'm not about to book a concert tour, but my new agent isn't pressing for one, either."

Piper laughed.

Then silence fell for several seconds. It wasn't an uncomfortable silence, but she felt like she wasn't supposed to break it.

"I wanted to offer to play at your wedding, if you'd like."

"Are you serious? I thought you didn't perform anymore."

"It's not a performance, it's a gift. I'm…" Cass's voice trailed off then she took an audible breath. "I'm working on a song for you both."

"As in composing us a song?" Piper asked in shocked awe.

"Um…yes. Is that all right?"

"That's fantastic. I don't know what to say. *Thank you* seems so inadequate."

"I'm really happy to do it. Zee helped Neo see what was important and stopped the stubborn idiot from breaking my heart."

"Zephyr did?" Piper asked in even more shock.

"Oh, yes. I think men are just smarter about other people's relationships than their own."

"Maybe not all men."

"But definitely our men," Cass said emphatically.

Piper wasn't sure she considered Zephyr hers even though they were getting married. "Is Neo smarter about others then?"

"He knew you were special to Zee the minute he told us he was bringing you to dinner. It took Zephyr considerably longer than a single comment to figure out you were special to him."

"I can't argue with that."

"Are things okay with you two?" Cass asked delicately.

"Better than. He may not love me, but he wants me and really wants me to be the mother of his children."

"*You* do love him, though."

"So much."

"That's good. I think Zee deserves lots of love and a very special woman like you. Maybe he'll learn to trust in love by living with it and the positive results of it on a daily basis."

Piper was certainly hoping that was the case. "Thank you. Ditto Neo about the love of a special woman, even though I've just recently become convinced he's human."

Cass's laugh was sweet and light. "Don't worry. He just figured that out himself recently."

"You're awfully good for him."

"And you're fabulous for Zee."

"I'll try to be," Piper promised.

"Just be you...that's all he seems to need."

And even without the love, Piper thought Cass just might be right.

She had to hope so, because losing Art had devastated her. Losing Zephyr would kill her.

The day sped by as Piper tried to catch up on her work while still coming to terms with the huge changes in her life. Little more than two weeks ago, she had just acknowledged the fact that she had fallen in love with a man who, while having sex with her, did not consider himself her lover. Now, she was pregnant with his baby, engaged to be married and moving in with him.

Love her or not, she trusted Zephyr to be faithful. Her billionaire tycoon was nothing like her ex.

If anything, she felt like she was the one luring Zephyr into marriage under false pretenses. Only she wasn't. She'd told him she loved him, so it was no secret she had to feel guilty about. Just because she was getting the deepest desire of her heart, or at least its twin, didn't mean she was taking advantage of anyone. Zephyr wanted to marry her; he wanted their baby as much as she did.

No matter how fortuitous this pregnancy was for her, giving Piper a chance at a lifetime with the most amazing man walking, she had not gotten this way on purpose. Zephyr knew it, too. He even felt responsible.

So why did she still feel as though she was pulling a fast one on him?

Maybe because she knew with absolute certainty that Zephyr would not be marrying her if she *wasn't* pregnant. And she wasn't offering to wait until the iffy first trimester was over, was she?

No.

On top of all that, he had offered her the option of moving to Greece and living on a private island. Was it any wonder she felt like she'd been dumped in a waking dream?

Merely accepting the fact that she was pregnant was hard enough. She didn't feel any different, but the blood test assured her that she would be soon. Her hand slid to her still flat stomach while she clicked the print function on the presentation she'd just finished.

Brandi had done a lot of the preliminary work and it had only been a matter of changing a few things before it was ready for presentation. Thank goodness. Piper's mind was scattered to the four winds.

But scattered or not, there was one thing she was sure of: they would be happy together. If she didn't believe that, she would not be moving in with him, much less marrying him. But she did believe it, deep in her bones. He was perfect for her, even if he had a mental block where love was concerned. And she was perfect for him.

No matter how much everything else scared her, she had to cling to that knowledge.

And right now she had to work.

Giving a final read-through to the design proposal for a

local private attorney's office space, she left her office and headed toward the shop floor in search of her assistant.

"Hello, Pip."

Piper's head snapped up at the male voice she had not heard since leaving New York.

Wearing a designer suit from last year's line and looking years older than the last time she'd seen her ex-husband, Art Bellingham stood not five feet in front of her.

"What are you doing here?" she blurted out, her usual professional persona deserting her completely.

"An old friend can't drop by to visit?" He tried the smirking half smile she used to find so sophisticated, but now just seemed cheesy.

"You are not an old friend."

"That hurts, Pip. We were friends once." Now he was laying on the charm.

It wasn't working, not even sort of. She shook her head, clearing the cobwebs old memories had spun so quickly the moment she heard that annoying old nickname, and then looked around for her assistant, Brandi. Watching Piper and Art with avid interest, her twenty-two-year-old assistant was standing near a display of sample drapery fabrics.

Piper held the design proposal out to her. "Put this in presentation format and get the color boards we made to go with it. You'll be presenting it to the client at tomorrow morning's meeting."

"You sure I'm ready for that, boss?" Brandi asked, her focus now completely on the designs in her hands.

"Yes." The younger woman had done supervised presentations with aplomb. She was ready to fly solo.

"Fab! I'll get right on this." She rushed toward their work corner.

That took care of one distraction.

"Is this a business or social call?" Piper asked Art, feeling more in control of herself.

"A little of both, Pip."

"My name is Piper. I hate that nickname. I always did." And he'd always insisted on using it.

"Hey, don't get all offended." He put his hands up in mock supplication. "It's not always easy letting go of the past."

She crossed her arms and gave him a look she had learned from Zephyr when he dealt with particularly irritating suppliers. "Funny, after the way you blackballed my name in the New York interior design industry, I had no problem leaving my past behind."

"Is that why you sicced your billion-dollar pit bull on me?" He frowned and shook his head, signs of his disappointment that had affected her at one time like an arrow to the heart.

Now she felt nothing but some amusement that he thought the guilt card could *ever* work between them again. "I don't know what you are talking about."

"I was hurt when you walked away from our marriage. I may have said some things that could be taken in a detrimental way," he said like he was sharing some big confidence, "but that's no reason for you to destroy a design firm that's been in my family for three generations. I thought better of you, Pip—*Piper*, I really did."

His guilt trip attempts were getting old fast. "I repeat…I do not know what you are talking about." She tapped her sandal-clad foot. "Start making sense, or take your smarmy self out of my shop."

"*Smarmy?* Piper, is that really how you see me?"

"That wounded look stopped working before our marriage did, and I don't think you want chapter and verse on how I see you, Art."

He looked startled for a moment and then sighed. "You may be right about that. Look, I understand you having some sour grapes toward me, I really do."

"That's big of you."

He frowned. "But not my company. You built a name for yourself with Très Bon."

Seriously? He was going to use *that* argument about this—whatever this was. "A name that you dirtied with your rotten, not to mention *untrue* slurs."

"I told you, I was smarting from our breakup. I exaggerated some things. I wasn't myself."

"You made stuff up with the creativity of a fiction writer."

He grimaced. "You may have a point."

She was so done with this conversation. "So, you're here to apologize?"

"If that's what it takes."

"To do what exactly?" Piper asked, still bewildered as to what her ex was talking about.

"To get me off Zephyr Nikos's most wanted list."

Now, that was unexpected. "*Zephyr?* What has he got to do with you, or Très Bon for that matter?" Très Bon was not the type of design firm Zephyr used on his projects. They lacked the innovative approach he considered a must.

"He's been blackballing my company in circles that have debilitating influence."

"You don't honestly believe I convinced him to blackball you?" Piper asked, deeply offended. "You know me better than that."

"I thought I did, but a man like that wouldn't go after me without motivation. I'm beneath his notice." And didn't it pain Art to admit it?

"If he's been slandering you, why haven't you filed a lawsuit?"

"Right, like the man would be stupid enough to say anything he could be held liable for in a court of law."

"That's the first thing you've said that makes any sense. Zephyr is a very busy man. Why would he take even a few minutes from his jam-packed schedule to besmirch your company's vaunted reputation?"

"Ask him! All I know is that Très Bon is on the verge of bankruptcy and it's all that bastard's fault."

"First, don't you ever insult Zephyr Nikos in my presence again. He's a hundred times the man you are, or could even hope to be. Second, if you're on the verge of bankruptcy, it has more to do with the way you run your business on the edge of overextension and always have done."

"His smear campaign has cost me business!" Art insisted.

"Campaign? Now I know you're lying. Zephyr simply would not waste that much time on you."

Zephyr enjoyed Piper's staunch defense, but it was time to step in. "For a man in my position, it only takes a comment here and there," he said as he walked around the personalized paint chip display that blocked his view of Piper and Art.

Piper's expression lit up as she unfolded her crossed arms and gave him a bright smile. "Hi, Zee. I didn't know you were stopping by."

"I got word Arthur Bellingham was in Seattle." He gave the other man a once-over, not impressed with what he saw. Piper had been married to this? "I had a feeling he'd come crying to you rather than be a man and face me himself."

"Be a man?" Art asked in outrage. "I've never even met you, Mr. Nikos. How would I get an appointment?"

"Did you try calling my secretary?"

Art checked as if the idea had not occurred. "No."

"She has instructions to put your call through."

"You've given your secretary instructions about Art?" Piper asked, clearly attempting to assimilate that knowledge with her heretofore stated belief Zephyr had nothing to do with the shift in Très Bon's reputation. *"You had some kind of travel alert set on him, too?"*

Zephyr shrugged, not as relaxed as he wanted to appear. "I am a thorough man."

"You're a petty tyrant, is what you are," Art said, blotchy color rising in his face.

The man was every bit the idiot Zephyr had thought him. "Calling me names isn't the best way to try to get on my good side."

"Once you've set a course of action, you don't change it. There is no getting on your good side," the dissipated-looking designer huffed.

"I almost have to respect your foresight in not trying the rational one-businessman-to-another approach."

"Once I realized you were the man behind the fall of my company's reputation in the international development community, I did my research. Words like *stubborn, highly intelligent, ruthless* and *deceptively charming* are used to describe you. *Reasonable* is not."

"But I am a reasonable man."

"You always have been with me," Piper agreed with a smile.

"Of course you would say that," Art sneered. "You two are obviously having an affair."

"We are engaged to be married," Zephyr said in dangerous tones the other man would do well not to ignore, "not having an affair."

"Well, congratulations." Sarcasm dripped from every syllable.

"Thank you." Zephyr did sardonic truth up there with the best of them. "That happy news aside, I did not express my less than favorable opinion of your unimaginative and overpriced design firm for Piper's sake."

"Right," Art said sarcastically.

"Had you not done your level best to destroy not only your marriage, but also any hope of ongoing friendship with Piper as well, she probably would never have left New York."

"That's true," Piper added with a look that could only be termed sentimental.

Zephyr smiled at her. "I'm glad you came to Seattle."

"Me, too."

Art made a disgusted sound. "And you're trying to say you did not destroy my company because of her."

"Only indirectly. I demand the best, isn't that right, *yineka mou*?"

Piper nodded, looking no less perplexed. "Yes."

"You are the best."

"Thank you." Her lovely blue eyes began to gleam with understanding.

"If I had gone with the recommendation of one of my colleagues based on things he had heard as a result of Arthur Bellingham's very real smear campaign against you in New York, I would not have hired you for that first job."

"But you didn't."

"No, I spoke to local clients you had worked with and visited properties you'd finished, but most importantly, I liked the proposal you gave me for my own project better than anyone else's," Zephyr disclosed.

"So, what was the problem?" Art demanded, showing a real lack of understanding his offense, even after Zephyr explained it.

"Your lies almost cost me the work of a fantastic designer."

"So, you decided to destroy my business?"

"Are you an idiot? I did not destroy your business. I merely helped you along in the process." But would Piper see it that way, as well?

"You utterly *ruthless* bastard!" Art rasped in a low voice.

He could not deny it. He was ruthless and he was a bastard. His only real concern was how his new fiancée responded to this particular truth. "At least I'm an honest one. Unlike your creative dealing with the truth, I never once said something about your firm that wasn't true. I *wouldn't* hire Très Bon for one of my properties. You *are* overextended financially and have been for years. Your designs *are* unimaginative. And *you do* have a reputation for finishing a project over budget and late."

Art sniffed superiorly, an effort that was completely wasted on his audience. "That has never bothered my clients in the past."

"You mean they tolerated your shoddy business practices in order to attach the name of Très Bon to their buildings."

"It was a name worth having before you set out to destroy it."

"Your uncle and grandfather ran a decent, if conservative design firm. You've been doing your best to destroy their work with bad business decisions since taking over ten years ago."

"Don't you care about the people that are going to be out of work when Très Bon folds?" the other man asked, appealing to Piper, rather than Zephyr.

But it was Zephyr who answered. "Did you care about Piper having to leave New York, her career in tatters?"

"She's just one person!"

Yes, definitely an idiot. "And you lied about her."

"I *knew* it was about Pip."

Zephyr winced at the name and looked at Piper. "Do you like that ridiculous nickname?"

"No. I already told him not use it, but as usual with Art, he didn't listen to me." She sounded mildly annoyed, but it was the lack of expression on her face that concerned Zephyr.

"If he had, his business might not be in trouble right now."

"She left, not me!"

Piper frowned at her ex, but no real anger shined in her eyes. "I left because you cheated on me and then fired me when I filed for divorce." There was no real heat in her words, just a weary-sounding truth.

Art's glare wasn't so insouciant. "You didn't used to be vindictive."

"I'm not vindictive now."

"Then get him to stop." Art contrived to sound desperate and pleading. He even said, "Please."

Zephyr barked out a laugh and she looked at him with a question in her eyes. "Your ex is quite the actor."

"Oh, I think he's every bit as despairing as he sounds and frankly, I understand why," Piper responded.

"You feel sorry for him?" Zephyr demanded incredulously, his worry ratcheting up a notch.

"I know what it's like to have your career ripped away by the careless words of someone else. I'd never wish that on even my worst enemy."

"I have no problem wishing it on him," Zephyr admitted in the spirit of complete honesty.

"Obviously." She did not sound particularly condemning, but nor did she sound approving.

He couldn't help morbidly wondering if their relationship was going to survive the revelation of the ruthless aspect to his nature. Though was it a revelation? She'd known his plans to fight for majority custody without him ever having to voice them.

Zephyr turned cold eyes onto the other man. "What did you hope to gain by coming here?"

Art looked like he was trying to decide how honest to be. Finally, shoulders slumped, he said, "Ideally Piper would convince you to say you'd been mistaken about my firm."

"I do not lie." And he sure as hell hoped she would not ask him to.

"I'd settle for you calling off the dogs." Like he had any room to negotiate.

That was the most the other man could ask from Zephyr, but the request came with an inherent error in thinking. "I have not set any dogs on you. I did not have to." It really had been just a comment here and there.

He certainly hadn't offered favors for passing the word along.

"So you've implied. Everything is my fault, according to you."

"That is how I see it."

"So, you aren't going to do anything to help me?" he asked Piper rather than Zephyr once again.

This time Zephyr let her answer.

"I don't know what I can do," she said.

"You could come back to work for Très Bon."

It was all Zephyr could do not to bark out a decisive, "Hell, no," but he respected and trusted Piper to get the point across on her own.

"Not in this lifetime." There wasn't even an ounce of maybe in her voice.

Art waved his hand, dismissing her denial. "Think about it, we can open up a West Coast office and you can head it up."

"I'm not even flirting with interested." Piper was no slouch at sarcasm herself.

"Then, I guess there's nothing to do but claim bankruptcy and lay off all of Très Bon's employees."

Zephyr's disgust meter reached red levels. "Don't be a melodramatic ass. A halfway decent management consultant could pull your company out of the red with a stringent reorganization and consolidation of resources."

"Not if you keep blacklisting us."

Zephyr flicked a look at Piper and then back to the other man. "In future, you tell the truth about Piper's talent and abilities and I'll do my best to avoid having to tell the truth about yours."

"I guess that's the best I'm going to get."

"I could suggest a consultant for your reorg." See him be reasonable.

"I'll find my own consultant and my own way out." Art turned on his heel, his former bravado pulled around him like a tacky suit, and left.

"Man, you guys are better than the soaps," Brandi said, a color board in each hand. "I just wanted to check these were the ones we planned for this design."

"Yes, those are the ones." Piper rubbed her forehead, fatigue clear on her features. She had not gotten enough sleep the night before to make up for her sleepless night away from him. "I'll be gone for the rest of the day. If you need to contact me, call my cell."

"Like always, boss. No worries." She went back to the work area.

Piper sighed. "She thinks she's Aussie and she's never even been out of the States."

"The idea of moving to Greece should appeal."

"If I asked her to, I'm sure it would."

That did not sound good. Something cold settled in his gut. "So, you are not planning to ask?"

"I've done all the discussing of my private life in my place of business I want to for today. Let's go."

He wasn't about to argue. If she was going to tell him she had changed her mind about marrying him, he would rather hear it somewhere he had a chance at changing her mind. Somewhere private.

When they got to her apartment, Zephyr had his emotional game face on. The one that showed nothing except humor when he wanted it to. Piper wasn't sure what made him draw into himself like that, but she wasn't going to let the visit from Art drive a wedge between them. If seeing her ex had done one thing, it had driven home to her how lucky she was to have a man like Zephyr in her life now.

His sense of justice was a little overdeveloped, but that was better than being a man who not only lied to others, but also to himself. Like Art.

Thinking how to best handle the emotionless vibes coming off her sexy fiancé, she sighed and stopped in front of her door. "We forgot something when you came into my shop earlier."

"What was that?" he asked with a weariness she did not understand.

"To kiss."

"You want me to kiss you?"

He really had to ask? "Yes."

"I can do that."

"It wouldn't say much for our upcoming nuptials if you couldn't," she sassed.

Morphing into a sensual predator before her eyes, he pushed her against the apartment door with his body, one hand on either side of her head. "You know what I've noticed lately?"

"No, what?" Was that breathless voice hers?

"You've got a real thing for getting the last word."

She would have answered that, but his lips were in the way.

CHAPTER EIGHT

AND very nicely, too. She loved this side of him and didn't really care what that said about her.

He didn't rush the kiss and neither did she. Of one accord, they broke apart to turn together to unlock and open the door. Once through, Zephyr made sure it was shut and locked again before leaning back against it with her in front of him.

His hold said one thing. Talking could wait. Everything but this intense pleasure between them *would* wait.

He leaned down and sucked up a pleasure mark on her neck while his hands skimmed down the front of her body, only to sweep up again, bringing the hem of her shirt along the way. His fingertips brushed against the smooth skin of her torso.

She writhed against his hard body, reveling in the feel of his erection pressing into her back. "Yes, Zee, touch me."

His hands cupped her breasts, squeezing lightly in nothing short of a tease.

"More, you know I want more." And he loved it when she told him so. She'd discovered that fact early in their relationship.

"Do you, *yineka mou*?"

"You know."

He kissed all around her ear and whispered, "Oh, yes, I do know."

His hands slid inside her bra to play with her nipples as he nibbled on the supersensitive spot behind her ear, laving shimmering nerve endings with his tongue.

She pressed back against him harder, her feminine center aching for the attention he was showing to the rest of her body.

Proving he was really adept at reading her mind, one of his hands moved down to undo her trousers. Her body knew what that meant and hot liquid gushed between her legs as her entire body thrummed with a new level of nascent desire. He pushed fabric down her hips without ceremony along with her panties. She stepped out of the pile of blue linens and silk, not caring that she still wore the high-heeled sandals she'd had died blue to match this particular outfit.

His rogue hand slid right over her mound and then long, knowing fingers were playing a symphony on her clitoris, drawing it into swollen sensitivity.

She arched toward the touch, a mewling sound that would have embarrassed her if she was not so turned on coming from her throat. He played her right through to a shocking, intense, early orgasm.

Only then did he start taking his own clothes off. It all got really hectic then and somehow she ended up leaning, with her hands on the back of the couch, her legs spread, and still wearing her heels.

He pushed his big sex into her now pulsing depths, eliciting moans and groans from her as well as unrestrained pleas for more, more and more.

So darn good. "How can it always get better?"

"I don't know. I don't care." He started a driving rhythm that would have sent her right over the back of the couch if he didn't have both arms around her.

One hand continued to toy with her breasts and stomach while the other kept up constant stimulation to her clitoris.

She was screaming with her second orgasm as he roared out his climax inside her, long, sweaty, strenuous minutes later.

Afterward, he cajoled her into the shower, where they washed each other with as much pleasure as making love. She adored the domestic intimacy of showering together. It was one of the things that said most clearly to her that they were a couple.

They were making dinner together in her small kitchen when he said, "I thought you were going to back out of marrying me."

So, that was what had him behaving strangely earlier. "For heaven's sake, why?"

"You have seen my ruthless side and what it can lead to."

"I always knew you could be ruthless, but I have to admit I have a hard time reconciling the man I've come to love with one who would set out destroy someone else's reputation." She leaned up to kiss his jaw.

He turned away, tension radiating in every inch of his six-foot, three-inch frame. "You never asked me about my father."

"You know who your biological father is?" she asked in shock. She'd just assumed his mother had not known which of her clients had sired her oldest son.

"Yes."

"Well, don't make a meal of it." She pulled him around to face her. "Tell me."

"If you talked to the other men of his class, they would tell you he was a respected olive grove owner from an honorable family who was lucky in his investments. Only he and his wife had luxurious tastes in living that could not be supported with his olive income. He made investments, but not of the re-spectable kind."

"What do you mean?"

"He invested in a stable of women, and yes, that is what he called them. He treated them as well as he would horses, I suppose. He provided for their physical needs, while expect-ing them to serve his customers. And him. My mother was his favorite. He was the only man allowed to copulate with her without using a condom."

"He kept her working for him, even after she had his son?" What a prince...*not.*

"He did not recognize me as such. Not until I was older and he realized his legitimate wife was never going to give him an heir for the family's grove. He came to the home with the intention of claiming me. He thought I would be grateful he wanted to 'adopt' me."

"What a morally corrupt, not to mention selfish, *slimeball*." Her heart ached for the child Zephyr had been and for the man whose ability to trust and love had been so damaged.

"That's how I saw it. I had no intention of playing dutiful son to a man who treated my mother like a commodity and was content to leave me in an orphanage for years."

"That's when you and Neo ran away from the home, isn't it?"

"Yes. He'd had much looser restrictions on him while living with his mother, before she died. The home felt like a prison to him."

"So, you two took off together."

"And helped each other build lives as far from the ones we'd been born to as it was possible to get."

"You both succeeded admirably."

"Yes."

But she was still interested in what had made him go tense. "So, you brought your dad up for a reason right now."

"You are right." He sighed and tried looking away again.

She wouldn't let him. "Tell me."

"When I was in a position to do so, I made sure the truth of his *investments* was brought to light."

Ah, that made sense. "That ruthless side of yours showing itself."

"Yes."

"Did he go to jail?"

"*Ohi*…no, he had money. He paid his way out of trouble, but he couldn't pay his respectable wife to stay with him. In a true twist of irony, he ended up married to one of his prostitutes and she's given him two children. Both daughters. She rules the home every bit as *ruthlessly* as he used to rule his 'stable.'" He stopped, his body going rigid, an expression of horror crossing his features. "We are not inviting them to the wedding. The girls are too young to know who or what I am and I have no interest in recognizing that pimp as my father."

She shuddered. "Don't worry, I wouldn't even consider it."

Relief showed on his face. "So."

"So?"

He looked at her like he couldn't quite figure out what was going on in her head. Since that was usually her role, she got an inappropriate little thrill from seeing the shoe on the other foot for a change.

"I am a very ruthless guy." He made it sound like that was some big revelation.

"It's a little disturbing," she said, unable to resist the urge to tease a little.

"Disturbing enough to make you question your decision to marry me?"

She refused to treat this like a serious question. "That depends."

"On what?"

"On whether there are any other people you feel the need to 'tell the truth' about." She fluttered her eyelashes at him, making it clear that she was joking.

He, however, looked as serious as a heart attack. "No."

"I was joking, Zee. I'm not really worried about it. Nothing I learned today changed in any way how I feel about you." She spelled it out for him because he seemed to need that.

"You do not think I am like my father?"

"What?" She grabbed his shoulders and tried to shake him. It didn't work, him being the buff stud that he was, but he got the idea. "How could you ask that? You are nothing like that user."

"But he is ruthless about getting what he wants."

"And you are ruthless in standing for the truth. That can be overwhelming at times and a great burden to bear at others, but it's as far from the man who exploits the weakness of others to provide for his own ill-gotten luxuries as the life you now live is to the one you were born to." She needed him to see that.

"I did not want him punished for what he did to me, but I wanted his world to see him for who he was and how he took advantage of others."

"I know."

"He destroyed too many lives."

"And I bet he was never sorry he did so. He and Art have more in common than you and him."

"Too bad they are not related."

"Yes, it is. Art's family are decent, nice people. I have no idea how he turned out so selfish and blind to his own faults."

"My mother did not want to give me up. Even when I was a small boy, I understood that. She felt she had no choice. She did not want me to be raised in a whorehouse."

"So, she chose the lesser of two evils, and paid the rest of her life for having to do so."

"I think you are right." He looked like he was having a revelation.

"It's that mother-to-be oracle thing again," she teased.

He smiled and then went serious again. "That is why you want to invite her to the wedding. You think it is time she stopped paying."

"I think it is time you both stopped paying for things that cannot be changed."

"I will call her tomorrow."

"Thank you."

Zephyr stared at his computer monitor. It displayed his latest project spreadsheet, but all he saw was an image from the past—his mother's face one of the many times she told him she loved him before leaving him at the home. He could see something in that mental picture that he had never let himself acknowledge before, the terrible pain in eyes so like his own.

His burned and he blinked rapidly.

"At Last" by Etta James started playing in that tinny way that ring tones did, bringing him firmly into the present.

He grabbed his cell phone and pressed the talk button without looking at the screen. "Hello, *pethi mou*."

What he lacked in sentiment, Piper made up for. She'd programmed the song into his phone as her personal ring tone after agreeing to marry him. She was going to go all gooey-eyed over the wedding ring set he had ordered to be overnighted from Tiffany's. He'd had their names and the date they met engraved on the inside. It was such a little thing, but it would be special to her.

"How did it go?" Piper asked without preamble.

"She cried."

"You're not surprised."

"No." Not after Piper had warned him to expect it. "We agreed to meet for dinner on a day before the wedding, as you suggested." Piper had thought him seeing his mother for the first time in more than two decades at his wedding might be too much drama.

He'd agreed for his mother's sake. If he thought he might be grateful for it, too, he wasn't saying.

"Great. Are we meeting at a restaurant?"

"No, she asked us to come to her home," he replied.

"And you agreed?"

"Yes."

Piper was quiet for a second and then asked, "Will her husband be there?"

"Yes." He might as well get it all out at once. "He's coming to the wedding as well."

Absolute silence met that bombshell.

"He wanted to talk to me, too."

"What did he want to say?"

"That he was very, very, *very* sorry. That he was wrong to make my mother let me go. He said he wanted to tell me before, but he could not until I was ready to talk to him. He cried, too."

"I've heard Greek men do that sometimes."

"Not expatriates."

"Of course not." There was a teasing note in her voice, but he did not call her on it.

"I heard the story of how my sister and brother learned of my existence."

"Really?" The sound of Brandi asking a question in the background came over the phone. Piper covered the mouthpiece and he could hear the muffled sound of her answer before she said, "I thought it was odd your mother told them after not allowing you to see them once they were old enough to remember you."

"You never considered I might have told them?"

"No."

"Even with my ruthless streak?"

"Like I told you, it's a good kind of ruthlessness."

"You have a great deal of faith in me."

"Yes, I do."

His heart contracted at her words, but he ignored the strange sensation and said, "Iola found my mother crying over a pile of old photos. They were of me. My sister convinced our mother to spill the whole story."

"She must be pretty persuasive."

"She is very stubborn."

"Like her brother, hmm?"

"Perhaps."

Piper laughed. "There is no *perhaps* about it."

"You are treading on thin ice here."

"I like to live dangerously." Her smile carried in the sound of her voice.

"I can tell."

"How old was she when your sister found out about you?"

"Twelve. She was furious with her father. She called him

a monster and refused to speak to him at all for an entire year after finding out about me."

"Wow, she might even be *more* stubborn than you."

"You think?" He had always enjoyed the fact that to Piper, he was just a guy she could joke with, not someone she was too in awe of to treat like a human.

"I'll have to consider it."

"She never told me about all that once I contacted them. She let me believe my mother told her of her own volition, which in a way, she had. Iola did not want me to hate our mother."

"She also respected the distance you maintained. It's pretty obvious she felt you had the right to set the terms for your relationships with your family."

"Yes." And he had always appreciated that.

"Are you okay?"

"Naturally." A simple conversation with his mother and her husband wasn't about to disconcert him. Although, maybe there hadn't been anything simple about that phone call.

"You are the most amazing man, do you know that?" The warm approval in Piper's voice washed over him.

"You've said something to that effect before."

"Well, I mean it even more now," she assured him.

"You are good for my ego, even if I do not understand why you are so impressed."

"It took a lot to forgive your mom and her husband."

"I forgave them a long time ago." A man could not afford to expend the energy to maintain anger and hatred when he was building a new life for himself. "I simply did not trust them to be a positive part of my life. You have convinced me to give them a chance."

"I love you, Zephyr."

"Thank you."

She laughed. "You are welcome. I still say it takes a big man to overlook the sins of the past and forge new relationships in the present."

"I am glad you think so." He liked looking heroic in her eyes.

"So, our families are all going to be there. Tell me you got the church booked."

"Since we were flexible what day of the week we would be married, it was no problem. My secretary is booking your family's flights even as we speak. They will all arrive over the weekend, which will give them time to take in some sights before our wedding blessing on Thursday evening. We will fly over to Greece with Neo and Cass on the company jet after their wedding on Sunday."

"I'm still having trouble taking in the fact we'll be married in just over two weeks. In Greece, just like I dreamed."

"It is what you wanted." And what he had wanted for himself as well.

"So you made it happen."

"If a little unorthodox in my methods."

They had discovered that having the actual wedding in Greece required a lot of paperwork that would extend the date for their ceremony further out than they wanted. Neo had suggested a civil ceremony in Seattle followed by a blessing in Greece, for their families to attend. When Piper agreed, Zephyr had insisted on coordinating both events immediately.

"I kind of like it this way. The legal ceremony is private, just for us, and our families get to share in the communal blessing."

"As long as you are content so am I," Zephyr responded.

"Just keep saying stuff like that."

She was always so positive and it had only gotten better since they decided to get married. A man could be forgiven for being impressed with his own acumen in choosing such a woman to marry.

"How goes the great search for a dress?"

"Splendidly, thank you. I found the absolutely most perfect one ever online. The designer is shipping it to a downtown bridal shop in case any alterations are needed."

"Good."

"It's going to cost more than the GNP of a small country." He could tell she was striving to feel guilty and failing miserably. She must *really* love the dress.

"I do not care." He wanted everything perfect for her and he was only grateful she did not want a huge event that would require months of planning. Months in which she could change her mind about marrying him.

Or, God forbid, lose the baby and destroy his chances of getting her to marry him at all.

"So you said." She sighed happily. "Thank you."

"You are welcome."

"Are you sure we aren't rushing?"

Something clenched in his gut. "Are you having second thoughts?"

"No! Not at all."

Okay, so that was good. "Have you changed your mind about walking down the aisle with a noticeable bump?"

"Definitely not."

"Then we are not rushing things, we are simply being expedient."

"Right. Um, Art called a little bit ago."

Was that what had prompted her uncertainty? If so, was it because old feelings for her ex had resurfaced, or was it because seeing him made her question her decision-making skills when it came to marriage? "What did he want?"

"It finally sank in what you said about us getting married."

"He is not invited." Forgiving his family was one thing, her ex was a bridge too far.

"He wasn't angling for an invitation, well not entirely."

"That man has no shame." And even less business sense.

"And you don't even know the main reason he called."

But it wasn't hard to figure out. "Let me guess. He wanted a loan?"

"Yes! How could he?"

"For a man like him? Very easily."

Piper made a sound of disgust that transferred more than adequately over the cell phone. "I suppose so, but there was a time, and I find this really hard to accept now without considering myself an idiot, only I loved that man—or at least the man I believed him to be."

"He has feet of clay."

"His whole body is clay, if you ask me."

Okay, so definitely not resurrected tender feelings. Zephyr could afford to be generous. "Do you want me to bail his company out?"

"Would you, if I did?" she asked, sounding more curious than anything.

"Yes."

"You didn't even hesitate."

"I want you to be happy."

"Even if I wanted you to do it, giving Art a loan would just be throwing good money after bad. Most of his best designers have left the firm because of creative or financial difficulties. I suggested moving to smaller offices when I still worked at the firm, but he liked the 'grand' impression the space made on clients, the illusion that the firm was bigger than it was. He's still paying rent on prime New York commercial real estate much bigger than he needs."

"He doesn't want to acknowledge his poor choices and the effect they've had on his company."

"He never did. As for all the employees that would be out of work, I made a few phone calls. Along with learning his best designers had left Très Bon, I discovered he's mostly been staffing with temporary interns since the year after I left. He always was more about appearances than substance."

"So, no loan?"

"No loan," Piper confirmed.

"I am sorry."

"So am I, for the people who do rely on Très Bon for their

livelihood and for his uncle, who is still living. Old Mr. Bellingham has to watch his company fall apart, but then he could have stepped back into the picture at any time. He gave acting control to Art, but never signed over his ownership of the company."

"So, your ex is *not* an issue between us."

"I told you he wasn't."

"You had feelings for him a long time after the divorce," he reminded her.

"You're right, but I got over him. With your help."

He didn't have to ask himself why that knowledge was so satisfying. "Where are we sleeping tonight?"

"My place. The movers are going to be there in the morning to pack me up."

"I look forward to sharing the same home." And for the first time, his penthouse apartment would be a home with her living there.

The move went smoothly and Piper was surprised at how easily her things integrated into Zephyr's apartment. It helped that he gave her carte blanche on the décor and over what furniture stayed and what had to go.

That could have made her feel like he didn't care how their home together took shape, but he noticed every change. And commented on it in some positive way. He'd just got through telling her how he liked the way her curtain scarves brought a splash of color to that side of the living room.

"Why are you staring at me like that?" he demanded.

"Like what?"

His eyes narrowed and she wondered if he'd say it. She knew what was in her eyes right now: love, adoration and even a bit of hero worship.

He was so perfect for her.

"Like I am the perfect man." Ah, he got it.

"Why wouldn't I?"

"No one is perfect, Piper."

"True, but then you don't have to be perfect for me to love you. You just have to be *perfect for me*. And you are."

He looked unconvinced, but he did not argue. "Did your dress arrive?"

"Yes."

"Who is the designer?"

"I'm not telling." His curiosity was cute, but if she told him that, he would be *so* offended. "You'll have to wait until our wedding blessing in Greece before you get to see me in all my glory."

"You aren't going to wear it for the civil ceremony?"

"Nope." She enjoyed teasing him about it. Who would have thought Zephyr Nikos would be so naff that he wanted to know what her wedding dress looked like? And he said he wasn't sentimental.

Right.

"I suppose you'll wear one of your work outfits to the courthouse, it being a weekday morning."

"I suppose you'll see when you get there." She adjusted the angle of the silk and bamboo screen she'd put in the corner.

"I don't plan to wear a blindfold on the way there."

"And I don't plan to spend the night in our apartment on Thursday."

That got his attention, and not in the fun way. "What? Why not?"

"Tradition."

"But…" He let his voice trail off, thought for a second and then gave her an immovable look. "Fine, but that tradition only gets one airing, do not think you are going to sleep anywhere but in our bed every night thereafter."

"Duly noted."

"I mean it, even the night before the wedding blessing in Greece."

She laughed. "Fine, but I'm leaving our bed early in the

morning and you're not going to see me until I walk down the aisle of the church again later that day."

"That is acceptable."

"I'm glad you approve." She sashayed over to him and wound her arms around his neck. "I know we're in a rush but I want to observe all the traditions that are important to you and me."

He pulled her in close. "No problem, just remember, no doubling up on traditions because we're having two ceremonies."

"But some traditions are worth doing twice, like the part where the officiant says, 'You may kiss the bride.' And I think having two wedding nights could be earthshaking. I even bought two different sets of sexy lingerie." She gave him her best fake disinterested look. "I suppose I could take one of them back."

Over her dead body.

"Let's not get hasty."

"So, you think—"

"That two wedding nights are worth two wedding ceremonies and all that entails."

She grinned up at him triumphantly.

"Except the sleeping apart thing. That's a one-time event."

"Agreed." It wouldn't be the same after the civil ceremony anyway.

Her family and his might not know they were already legally wed when they arrived in Greece, but she would.

"So, where are you going the night before our ceremony?"

"Cass invited me to stay with her and Neo. We're taking the limo to the courthouse. Neo is driving you."

"You've got it all planned, do you?"

"Any objections?"

"I could do without a night alone in an empty bed."

"You'll survive just fine." She gave him a small peck on the lips.

He returned it with interest before saying, "So you say. I probably won't sweep a wink."

"You'd better. I expect a wedding night to remember." As if he could give her anything but.

"*Every* night we spend together is one to remember."

"You know, for a man who staunchly denies any sense of romance, you do mushy awfully well."

CHAPTER NINE

"THE truth is not sentimental." Zephyr tried to look offended, but he was obviously pleased. Even if he didn't want to be.

"Whatever you say. I'm just glad I'm getting such a romantic guy to spend the rest of my life with."

Now, he was looking worried. "I don't do hearts and flowers, Piper. You know me better than that."

"Sometimes, I think I know you better than you know yourself." She could tell right away she shouldn't have said that aloud.

If Zephyr were a dog, his hackles would be at full attention. For a billionaire tycoon, he did a pretty fair imitation. "Like you knew Art?"

She understood where the question came from, but it still hurt. "I thought I knew my ex, but it turned out I only saw the man he wanted me to, until his whole facade came crashing down."

And she felt pretty gullible acknowledging that, but seeing Art again in person had made her realize just how much of who she thought he was had been a result of her imagination and his acting ability.

"You say you love me, but you have made me into some kind of superhero in your mind. What happens when you see me for the man I really am, unsentimental, ruthless tycoon and all?"

"First of all, I do see you for who you are, Zephyr Nikos." No matter how naive she had been with her ex, she hated that

Zephyr thought her judgment regarding him could be skewed. It was not the same at all. It wasn't. "We were friends before we were lovers," she reminded him. "I've seen you in every aspect of life from your most impatient day on the job to the moment when you realized your mom didn't give you up without immense regret."

"So?"

Sheesh, did he really think stuff like that didn't matter? But then not loving her, maybe it didn't to him. "So, I know you can be ruthless, but I also know you aren't obsessed with revenge. If you were, you would have done something to your mother's husband, but you never did. You bought them a house, put his children through school. You never did a single thing to hurt him. You're just not *that* ruthless."

"But I am."

"Oh, really?"

"You are being deliberately obtuse."

She pulled away from him, crossed her arms and glared. "No, that would be you."

"Is this our first fight?" he asked, as if the concept amused him.

She was not laughing. "No. We argued before." He was too fond of getting his own way for even their friendship to have been all smooth sailing.

And maybe so was she.

"Not since we got engaged." He tugged her toward the couch.

She put up token resistance, but grudgingly allowed herself to be maneuvered into a spot beside him. She refused to sit on his lap, however, and kept her arms crossed. "Considering how recent that is, that's not saying much."

"You said first of all."

"So?"

"That implies you have more to say on the subject. You might as well get it all out now."

Her first reaction was to accuse him of fishing, but then she realized this whole discussion might have taken the turn it did because he needed reassurance. And no way would Mr. Arrogant Alpha think to simply ask for it.

If Zephyr needed reassurance, she was happy to give it to him. Even if he was being more than a little annoying, but it was odd how she had told him she loved him and he was the one needing proof.

She was the one marrying a man who had told her he could not love her, and she had no fears she was not doing the right thing for her. Almost no fears. All right. Fine. *No fears she was willing to give voice to*. But what woman in her situation wouldn't be at least a little nervous?

"Maybe you aren't sentimental by nature, but you are just sappy enough for me, all right? You may not see yourself as romantic, but the way you are with me, the things you say and do, are all I ever wanted in that department. Art *pretended* to be the kind of man I could love. You are that man. You don't pretend to be anything. In fact, you are almost brutally honest at times."

"And that does not give you pause?" His tone doubted her sanity.

She did her best not to take offense. "No. Trust comes hard for me now. Knowing just how unwilling you are to lie, even when a lie would serve you well, is a great comfort to me. I *know* I can trust you, and I didn't think I'd ever be able to say that to a man I loved again."

"What is love without trust?"

"I don't know." Why didn't he ask her something easy like what the meaning of life was, or something? "I'm not a philosopher. I never pretended to be. All I know is that I do love you. I do trust you because of who you are. And nothing is going to change the way I see you. So, you might as well get used to it."

"I suppose I don't have much choice."

"Not if you still want to marry me."

"That is never up for discussion."

"Good."

"Can we progress to the makeup sex now?" he asked with a leer that should have irritated her.

But it just made her laugh. She uncrossed her arms.

"I think maybe we can."

They were soaking in a bubble bath after a tender session of lovemaking that had wrung every ounce of emotion and pleasure from her.

"I thought makeup sex was supposed to be all hot, sweaty and urgent."

"We have that without the lively discussions beforehand."

"True."

"Besides, I do not like to fit the stereotypes."

"No worries there. You are very much your own man, Zephyr."

"And you are a very special woman, Piper Madison."

"Be careful, you're sliding into sentimentality there."

"Then perhaps this is the ideal moment to do this."

"This?"

But he was leaning over the side of the oversized tub, reaching for something, and did not answer. When he straightened, there was a dark blue ring box with a white satin bow around it in his hand. There was no mistaking the signature look. He'd been shopping at Tiffany.

"Zephyr?" she asked in a voice that would not come out above a whisper in her suddenly dry throat.

He looked directly into her eyes, his espresso gaze both serious and warm. "Piper Madison, would you do me the honor of becoming my wife?"

He went blurry as happy tears filled her eyes and made her vision watery. "You know I will."

He took a gorgeous diamond-and-platinum engagement ring from the box and slid it onto her finger. "Every woman deserves a proposal before marrying."

"Thank you," she said in a choked voice.

"I knew you were going to go gooey on me."

She laughed. "That's me. Gooey."

"And incredibly sweet."

She swiped the water from her eyes. "I do love you."

"Wait until you see what I had done to the wedding rings." She grabbed for the box but he held it above his head. "No, no, no…not until the ceremony."

"You're just getting me back for my wedding gown."

"You yourself said I am not obsessed with revenge. I am merely revering tradition."

"You are revering a chance to keep me in suspense."

He shrugged. "Maybe."

"You…" She launched herself at him.

He tossed the box before accepting her weight as he wrapped his arms around her.

With frequent looks toward the street, Zephyr paced the landing at the top of the courthouse steps. He tugged at the neck on the white dress shirt he wore with the ring in his pocket. His gaze skimmed toward the building.

Neo lounged against the wall and watched him with a smirk.

Zephyr glared over at his closest friend. "You just wait. Come Sunday at the front of the church, *you* won't be so complacent."

"No, but I won't make a prat of myself pacing all over the sanctuary, either."

"I'm expending excess energy."

"And what do you call looking at your watch every thirty seconds? Checking the time?"

"They were supposed to be here five minutes ago."

"Are you seriously worried Piper isn't going to show up?"

"She wouldn't even let me text her last night." She'd said she wanted to observe the full tradition and he had indulged her.

He was an idiot.

Neo rolled his eyes. "Man, you have got it bad."

Zephyr refused to answer that silliness. "What I have is six minutes past the hour on my watch."

"And a bride arriving."

Zephyr spun around and sure enough, the limo was pulling up in front of the courthouse. An unreasonable amount of relief washed over him for the amount of time she was actually late, but she had left him once, if only for a week. And Zephyr knew better than most how easy it was to leave behind someone you professed to love.

The driver double-parked and turned on his flashers. Zephyr sprinted down the steps to open the door before the driver got around the car to do it.

Cass came out first, wearing a bright pink suit and a huge grin. "Happy wedding day, Zee."

"Thanks."

She stepped past Zephyr as he looked at his bride. And Piper looked like a bride.

She was wearing a short veil and a white cocktail-length dress with layers and layers of chiffon in the full skirt. Her blue eyes sparkled with a happiness he never wanted to see dimmed.

She put her hand out to him. "Help a girl out?"

Something went *twang* in his chest as he tugged her out of the limo and straight into his arms. Then, with a flip of her veil, he claimed her lips in a kiss he could no more have stopped than he could stop his own heartbeat.

The sound of honking horns and wolf whistles finally broke through to his consciousness and he reluctantly pulled back.

"I thought the kiss was supposed to come after the ceremony?" Cass teased.

Neo laughed. "We expatriate Greek tycoons do things our own way."

Piper looked up at Zephyr with passion glazed eyes. "I like the way you do things."

"Good. I have become set in my ways."

"You're a traditionalist with a twist." She sighed happily. "I like it."

"I like what you are wearing." She was right he was a traditionalist. He was more than a little pleased she had taken the effort to look like a bride for their legal ceremony. And such a beautiful bride.

She gave him a mischievous smile. "Wait until you see what I've got on under it."

He swore. "Do not say things like that."

"Why not?" she asked, all innocence.

"I do not fancy getting married with an erection in my pants." But he wasn't sure it was going anywhere, even if she refrained from all further naughty comments. He found the bridal look unbearably sexy on her.

"I can do that to you?" she asked teasingly.

"You know you can." Too damn easily.

"I'll try to be good."

"Not too good," he couldn't help saying as they headed up the steps arm in arm.

The ceremony was short and to the point. All the pomp and circumstance was being reserved for the church blessing in Greece.

So, the sense of profundity choking Zephyr as he signed the marriage certificate was totally unnecessary. However, it did not go away even as he handed the pen to Piper. Her hand trembled as she signed her own name and he didn't feel quite as foolish. This was a life-altering moment, after all.

They were now legally man and wife. She was his as no one had been since the day he walked through the children's home's doors.

He pulled her to him. "Is it time for the kiss now?"

"Yes, I do believe it is."

He tilted his head down and she met him halfway. Their lips met and clung in a kiss of promise.

He pulled his head back. "Mine."

"Yes, my personal caveman, I am yours. And you are mine." Her soft smile said she didn't mind his Neanderthal moments, but there was an emotion lurking in her azure eyes he did not understand. It was almost as if despite all her assurances to the contrary, linking her life to his frightened her on some level.

"Are you two sure you and Neo aren't blood brothers?" Cass asked with laughter. "You've got so many of the same primitive tendencies."

"We are brothers in every way that counts," Neo said with certainty.

Zephyr nodded his agreement.

"I guess that makes us sisters-in-law," Piper said to Cass with a happy smile.

Cass looked down at her own engagement ring with a satisfied grin. "Come Sunday we will be."

"I'm looking forward to it."

"Me, too."

"Right now, I'm looking forward to a champagne brunch back at the penthouse," Neo said. "My housekeeper has promised a repast fit for the superrich tycoons we are."

But it wasn't the penthouse they ended up in. Neo's housekeeper, Dora, was waiting for them in the lobby of the Nikos and Stamos Enterprises building, along with what looked like the majority of their employees. Big banners that read Congratulations Zephyr and Piper, and Congratulations Neo and Cassandra, hung on either side of the reception area. Black-clad waitstaff walked between groups of Stamos & Nikos Enterprises employees with black trays of food and silver trays of champagne.

Zephyr and Neo's personal assistants were standing together in front of the reception area. "Congratulations!" they said in unison.

"Ms. Parks, you planned this?" Cass asked in shock.

"With the help of Mr. Nikos's personal assistant and Mr.

Stamos's housekeeper, yes." The office automaton actually managed a smile for them all.

Dora rushed up and hugged first Neo and then Zephyr. "We wanted to do something to let you all know how pleased your employees are that you have both found personal happiness."

Cass hugged the housekeeper back and kissed her cheek. "Thank you. This is really special."

The older woman patted Cass's arm. "And you only stay as long as you are comfortable. Everyone understands. You are among friends here."

Several people who had gotten to know Piper when she worked on his projects came up to tell her how happy they were she'd finally made an honest man out of Zephyr. It was unreal. To hear them tell it, plenty of people realized there was something between them.

Of course, the sexual tension between them before they made love the first time had gotten pretty thick. And he hadn't made much effort to hide their intimate relationship afterward.

Neo took good-natured umbrage because he *hadn't* realized, though.

Zephyr just put his arm possessively around Piper's waist and enjoyed himself.

He received more good wishes at the surprise reception than he had over the entire course of his life. There were even gifts—appliances and the usual suspects in wedding presents as well as donations in all their names to area shelters that catered to families with children and to the foster care system.

"It's so perfect," Piper said in a tear-choked voice.

"I have always said we hire the best," Neo said smugly.

"Without doubt," Zephyr agreed.

The employees within earshot smiled, some laughed, and some even returned the compliment.

By the time he led Piper into their apartment a few hours later, an unfamiliar warmth suffused Zephyr's being.

"That was so nice of them," she said as she kicked off her wedding-white shoes.

"Neo was as surprised as I was."

"You had no idea they were planning anything?"

"None at all."

"Cass was shocked Neo's PA was in on it. She thought Ms. Parks hated her."

"I've often wondered if Ms. Parks is even human, but hate Cass? Who could? She's almost as sweet as you."

"You're being sappy again." Piper removed the short veil and tossed it toward the sofa. "I like it."

"And I like the idea of finding out what is underneath your wedding gown."

"Dress…it's a wedding dress. My wedding gown is ten times fancier. I feel like a modern-day royal in it."

"What was the name of the gown's designer again?"

"I didn't tell you and I'm not about to." She walked right into his arms. "I know you'd try to look it up on the designer's Web site."

"Smart, too." He cuddled her close. "Is it any wonder I wanted you for the mother of my children?"

"It's a good thing I got pregnant unexpectedly then, isn't it? You weren't going to do a thing about it." There was something in her tone he could not quite place.

"You know why."

"Yes, but I think we're both getting the long end of the stick on this marriage."

The relief he felt when she said that was all out of proportion.

"Even though I don't…" He didn't finish the thought, curiously unwilling to speak the words denying his love aloud.

So much for his vaunted honesty.

She shook her head, putting her hand up as if she would stop the words from coming out. "Don't say it. Not today. Not right now. I *do* and that's all that matters this minute."

It was not that easy. He knew it, but he could not deny her. "I need you." That had to be enough.

"Yes." With a flirtatious smile that masked something deeper, she put her hands behind her back. "More than you've ever wanted any other woman." Then he heard the sound of a zipper lowering.

His entire being took notice of that tantalizing sound. "In every way, you are unique in my life." That truth was one he could give her without apology.

"That is enough," she said as if she'd read his mind earlier.

"Is it?"

"Yes," she said fiercely. "Isn't it?" she almost demanded.

He nodded, unable to do anything but agree. "Yes. Enough. We are good together."

She did a little shimmy with her torso and her dress loosened. "We are *great* together." The white chiffon slid forward and down her arms. As it fell, it revealed the top of a baby-blue corselet that pushed her delicious breasts into mouthwatering prominence.

"Amazing."

"Together?"

"In every way."

She smiled that enigmatic smile women had been using on men since time immemorial and shifted her body just so. Air whooshed out of his lungs as the dress fell in a puddle of demure white chiffon at her feet, uncovering the rest of her scandalous unmentionables. The strapless corselet stopped just shy of her hips, leaving the tiny blue satin triangle of the thong she wore below it completely exposed. Her sheer stockings were held up midthigh with matching garters.

She turned in a slow circle, giving him a delectable view of her bare backside framed by the thin strings of her thong, tied together in a perfect little bow right in the center. Looking back over her shoulder, she winked and blew him a provoking kiss.

"You're an agent provocateur."

She gave that perfect peach of a bottom a little wiggle. "I try."

Once she was again facing him, she struck a pose that would have made a 1940s film vamp proud. "You like?"

"I—" His voice broke off in an embarrassing sound he refused to call a squeak. He cleared his throat. "I *adore*. *Yineka mou*, you are my favorite fantasy come to life."

"You've got a thing for pregnant women in sexy lingerie?"

"I've got a *thing* for you looking like a perfectly wrapped gift just waiting to be opened."

"You do seem to enjoy unwrapping me."

"I would have to be insane not to."

She sighed happily and licked her lips in what he would swear was an unconscious motion, despite her obvious attempt to provoke, and that just made the action all the more maddening. "I'm not a supermodel, Zee, but you have a way of making me feel like I could be."

Then that made them even, as she had a way of making him feel like a superhero. He put his hands out to her. "Come here."

She shook her head, the curls she'd put in her silky blond hair swaying against her shoulders. "Not yet."

"Why not?"

"You are wearing too many clothes."

"And you don't want to unwrap me?" he teased.

"Another time."

"You want me to undress for you."

"You know I do."

He did. If he had a tendency to unwrap her like a gift, she made no bones about the fact she got a lot of pleasure out of watching him undress.

He didn't have to do anything corny, like try to emulate a male stripper. Simply removing his clothes in his regular, methodical way could get her color up and turn her breathing erratic.

So, that was what he did. First, slipping out of his jacket and letting it lie where it fell on the floor. His tie came next, then the dress shirt that felt as constricting as a straightjacket.

He toed his shoes and socks off, then his slacks slid down his hips with a single shake before he stepped out of them. There was already a dark wet spot on the front of the black briefs that barely contained his erection, but he did not remove them.

They'd played this game before.

He put his arms out, offering himself for her pleasure. "How's this?"

"You're still wearing one last bit." A knowing smile teased her bow-shaped lips. She liked that last barrier to full disclosure.

"It's less than you."

She put her hand against her chin as if she was thinking that over. Then she shrugged and bent forward, giving him a tempting view of her breasts pressed so provocatively against the top of the corselet.

She stopped with her hands on one of her garters and looked up at him, sensual invitation glowing brightly in her azure eyes. "Did you want to do this?"

He did, oh, yes, he did. Without answering, he crossed the distance between them and then dropped to his knees in front of her. Gently, he brushed her hands away. "Mine."

"Yes, my caveman. Unwrap your very personal wedding pressie."

He slid the garter down her leg, caressing her shapely limb through the soft stocking as he did so. He did the other leg before returning to the original stocking to roll it down her thigh, over her calf and slip it off her perfectly shaped foot. "So beautiful."

"Thank you." Her voice was as hushed as his had been.

He removed her last stocking and then caressed up and down her legs. "Your skin is silkier than the stockings."

"Can't talk," she stuttered out as her knees tried to buckle.

He wrapped an arm around her waist to help her stand. "Is that bone in your corset?"

She'd worn this type of thing before and he'd loved it, but the stiffened fabric had never had anything unyielding sewn in its lining to give it form like the sexy number she had on right now.

"Metal. They're metal stays," she managed to say between panting breaths.

He wrapped his hands around her corseted waist, unexpectedly turned on even more by how it felt. "We're courting danger here. If I come in my briefs, blame your too-tempting self."

"You like the lingerie that much?"

"For the first time, I'm tempted to leave your sexy bits on while making love to you." There had been times he had not had the patience to get undressed, but he had never before wanted to keep an article of clothing on her while coupling their bodies.

"Whatever you want."

And damn if that didn't excite him even more.

"But this has to go," he said as he tugged the tie on the back of her thong and pulled the now useless triangle of silk away from her body.

He didn't wait for her to demand equal treatment before removing his own briefs, careful not to catch himself on the dark fabric stretched to capacity. Piper teased him about being oversized, but he thought he was just the right proportion for the tight heat that waited for him between her legs.

She reached out and caressed his length in one long stroke. They both shuddered at the contact. "Want you," she whispered wantonly. "Want this." She squeezed.

He groaned in preorgasmic pleasure. "You need to stop if you want that inside of you before it explodes like a Roman candle."

"More like Mount Vesuvius and I know you, you won't go soft. Not when you're like this."

"You're trying to kill me with pleasure."

She laughed, but the sound stuttered as he returned the favor, sliding his fingers between the wet folds of her sex. He tested the moisture and heat of her vaginal opening, pushing his middle finger far inside her and pressing right against the G-spot he'd spent a good long time acquainting himself with on previous occasions of intimacy.

"Oh, yes, Zee, right there."

He brushed his thumb right over the swollen nub of her pleasure and she squirmed and squealed. "Right *there*, *ne*?"

"Is this where the Greek endearments start?" she gasped out.

"They never stopped, *yineka mou*."

"What does that one mean? Cass seems to like it a lot."

"If you can think about Cass right now, I'm doing something wrong," he mock-growled.

Piper rode his hand with jerky movements. "Just tell me."

"My woman. Literally, now, *my wife*."

"You've always been more possessive than you wanted to admit."

"It's my Mediterranean blood."

She wrapped her arms around his neck, leaning up for a kiss that he didn't hesitate to give her. After several seconds spent in that pleasant pastime, she nuzzled his neck. "Make love to me, *husband*."

CHAPTER TEN

LEAVING their wedding finery in piles on the floor, he swept her into his arms and carried her into the bedroom with long, rapid strides. Once there, he changed his mind about using the bed and detoured to the armchair in the corner.

He sat down and then maneuvered her so she straddled his thighs.

She looked at him with passion-glazed eyes as she rubbed her wet, swollen nether lips against his achingly hard length. "Mmm…"

"Put your hands on the arms of the chair and don't let go," he instructed.

"But—"

"You said anything I wanted."

A sensual little laugh from her sent shivers of sensation through him. "I did."

When her hands were where he wanted them, he pushed up on her hips until she was spread open for him and completely accessible to his touch, but unable to pleasure herself without his cooperation. The fact she allowed him to control their lovemaking like this had his heart rate in the stratosphere and his sex harder than steel.

Her trust awed him, but all he wanted was to give her the maximum amount of pleasure possible. He began with her face, first trailing his fingertips along her cheekbones, jawline and then her lips. "Gorgeous."

She smiled, her lips parted on short panting breaths.

He kissed her, not deeply, just to let her know how much he loved that pretty curve of her mouth. Then he traced over where his fingertips had touched with his lips, then the barely there scrape of his teeth and finally laving each sensitized bit of flesh with the tip of his tongue.

He moved to her neck, caressing every susceptible spot on her nape, shoulders, upper back and chest he had spent so many hours discovering over the past months. She shivered as his fingertips skated over a particularly vulnerable spot between her shoulder blades.

"You play my body better than Cass plays the piano," Piper said on a low moan.

"I am obsessed."

"I believe you." She moaned again as his thumbs slid down inside the corselet and swept back and forth over her turgid nipples.

He kept up the caress, until they were such hard points they felt like pebbles against the pads of his thumbs. "Did it excite you to wear this under your demure little wedding dress?" he growled.

"You know it did." She loved wearing sexy things just for him, things no one else could see or know about but that he would discover when they were alone together.

"I remember the first time you left your panties off during the workday."

"You went ape-crazy when you realized that night in the hotel room."

He had and she'd laughed at him, at both his shock and his excitement, but not meanly. Only in pleasure of a secret shared, a bit of joke for his amusement.

This delectable outfit outdid the panty-free escapade by leaps and bounds.

She moaned and nodded as his mouth found that spot where her shoulder and neck joined that turned her into mush. "I was ready to make love long before the surprise reception was over."

"How did I get so lucky to end up with such a naughty woman?" he wondered out loud.

"I was never like this before." Her breath hitched as he gently bit down on the spot he enjoyed tormenting so much.

He lifted his head and looked at her. "No, this side of you is all mine."

"You're so possessive." She took a deep breath, clearly trying to gain control on her rampaging emotions. "Are you sure you don't have any dragons in your ancestry?"

"No mythical creatures, but maybe a conqueror or two. I am Greek." He had continued the caress of her nipples and breasts with his thumbs. It was enough stimulation to arouse, but not enough to satisfy and he knew it.

"You are incredible. Now, please…just…*please*, stop teasing me."

"I am not teasing you." No, he had every intention of following through on the promise of his touch. "I am driving you to the same frenzy of need roiling inside me."

"I'm already there."

"No, but you will be soon."

He arched up with his hips and used the steel rod between his legs to caress her intimate flesh.

She arched and cried out as his head brushed right over her swollen clitoris. "I want you inside me!"

"Soon." Before she had a chance to complain, he grabbed her corselet-covered waist and shifted her so the opening to her body was poised directly where it needed to be. He brought her down and surged up all in one movement, which elicited a scream of pure pleasure from her and a matching agonized groan from him.

Her restraint broke and she started rocking against him

with pure intent. He met her thrust for thrust until they climaxed together, their bodies caught in the rigor mortis of *la petite mort* for long seconds of bliss so complete, his vision went dark at the edges.

She collapsed against his chest, breathing so hard he got a little worried. He immediately started working on the ties of the corselet, getting it off of her faster than he was sure she'd managed to get into it.

The red marks where it had pressed into her skin were sexy, but he shook his head. "No more corselets or corsets, either, not until after the baby is born."

She fluttered her hand at him, so sated her eyes were mere slits of presleeping exhaustion. "Whatever."

"Thank you. You give the best gifts."

"I try," she slurred against his chest.

She was sleeping by the time he carried her to the bed and tucked her between the sheets, wrapping her securely in his arms.

Piper woke the next morning with a not-so-pleasant feeling of nausea. She groaned and swallowed convulsively as the sensation grew acute when she tried to sit up. She fell back on the bed, but that didn't help. Neither did Zephyr's big arm landing over her middle.

"Ugh…get off, Zee."

"Huh?" He sat straight up in bed, giving her a look of intense inquiry. The man was almost inhuman sometimes. "What is the matter?"

"The baby is finally making itself felt."

He frowned. "You look pale. Are you okay?" His brain seemed to catch up with his mouth and he asked, "What do you mean?"

"Morning nausea."

His expression cleared instantly and he jumped out of the bed with entirely too much energy. "I read about that. There are several recommendations, but the most popular is flat ginger ale and soda crackers. I've got some in the kitchen on standby."

"You've got flattened ginger ale on hand in the kitchen?" she asked, for the moment her incredulity winning over the morning sickness.

"Of course. It's Canada Dry, so there's actually ginger in the beverage. That's what is supposed to help. I've got the necessary inventory for the other suggestions as well, but let's try the crackers and pop first."

"Fine."

He was gone less than a minute before returning with a small package of saltines and a glass of amber liquid. "Take small sips and eat at least five crackers slowly before trying to sit up again."

She did and was thrilled when her next attempt to get out of bed was met with a much more mild form of queasiness. "It helped."

"Good. Now that you'll be sleeping with me every night, I can make sure you have what you need in the morning to keep from feeling too ill."

She smiled at his reiteration that there would be no more nights spent apart. "You've gotten spoiled to having me available for your nightlong cuddle." For a man who had never had a serious relationship, he was a professional cuddler.

"And I can watch over you."

"Right. This minute, you can watch me take a shower, or join me for one. Your choice."

She wasn't the least surprised when he was right behind her stepping into the decadently spacious glassed-in cubicle.

They spent the day enjoying their newly married status and packing for Greece. Everything was rosy until Zephyr had the realization that morning sickness might translate to airsickness. He paced their living room before dinner, reiterating his litany of worries and hinting that maybe they should change their plans.

That was not going to happen.

"I never get nauseated while flying," she tried to assure him.

"But now you have morning sickness."

"Which appears to be limited to mornings, for which I am very grateful."

"I'm thankful for that as well, but we cannot be sure—"

"And we can't prevent it happening by worrying about it, either."

"We should never have planned this wedding blessing in Greece."

Oh, he did not just go there. "You told me that you always expected to get married in Greece, no matter who you ended up married to." And she wasn't letting him lose that dream. Full stop. Period.

"Well, yes."

"And you know it is something I want, too. It just feels right, Zee. Besides, no way are we cancelling our plans now. Half my family is already there and your mom is dying to see you for the first time in decades."

"But—"

"I'm going to be fine. I promise." Man, if he was this bad now, what was he going to be like in the delivery room?

He'd probably demand the good drugs early. Which, come to think of it, was not such a bad thing.

"You cannot promise such a thing."

"I can. You'll be with me, so I know I'll be fine."

"I do not share your confidence."

"That's too bad, but we are not postponing the wedding blessing until I have to waddle down the aisle with a water-melon for a belly."

"Fine, but we will take a supply of soda crackers and flat ginger ale."

"Good idea. A Valium might be a good idea as well."

He stared at her in shocked disapproval. "You cannot take a Valium. It might hurt the baby."

"I wasn't thinking of the antianxiety meds *for me*."

* * *

The next morning was a repeat of the one before it, with the exception that after settling her tummy, Piper and Zephyr got ready to attend Neo and Cass's wedding.

It was a beautiful ceremony in one of Seattle's most traditional cathedral-style churches. Cassandra was a gorgeous bride in a gown with a long train and Neo looked exceedingly handsome in his tailored tuxedo. Zephyr stood up for Neo and one of Cass's first musical protégées acted as her attendant. Neo had invited his housekeeper and doctor. Cass had invited her new agent and a couple of her other former students. Other than Piper, there were no other guests at the formal wedding.

Unless you counted Cass's online friends, who were watching via the live feed from the camera placed on a tripod with a view of the aisle and altar.

Afterward, they all attended an intimate champagne brunch in a private room at one of Seattle's finest restaurants. Piper drank sparkling grape juice and enjoyed herself immensely.

Cass was so incredibly happy, so obviously in love and so very clearly certain of Neo's love that it brought tears to Piper's eyes. Neo didn't leave his bride's side for even a moment between the ceremony and when they left for his penthouse several hours later.

The next day, they were just as sweet. Neo held his brand-new wife's hand in their seats side-by-side on the company jet, while they waited to take off for Greece.

Since Zephyr had Piper's hand firmly clasped in his, she couldn't even work up a little emotional jealousy at the other woman's good fortune in being so obviously loved.

Zephyr might not love her, but if there was a difference in the way he treated her from the way Neo treated Cass, Piper could not see it. Maybe one day, that lack of love would show itself in ways that would hurt, but it wasn't now and Piper wasn't some drama queen who borrowed trouble from what might happen.

* * *

"You're pregnant, aren't you?"

Piper didn't even try to respond to her mother's question immediately. It was her first time alone with her parents since meeting up at the swank hotel Zephyr's secretary had arranged as their home base for the week of the wedding.

They were supposed to be relaxing together in the living area of Piper and Zephyr's palatial suite while Zephyr took a conference call in their bedroom. Afterward, they were going to have dinner together since the following night, Zephyr and Piper would not be available because they would be dining in his mother's home.

"It's not exactly a secret, Piper," her dad said when she didn't answer right away. "Why else would a billionaire marry you on such short notice?"

"Because he wants to?" she asked, feeling a little piqued her dad would put it that way.

"Does he love you, honey?" her mom asked.

"I love him, very much."

"That's what I thought. Did you get pregnant on purpose? Nothing good ever comes of machinations like that." Her mother sounded like a Victorian matron, not a modern woman with a daughter who was not only well past the age of making her own choices, but also already married and divorced.

"I did not," she replied hotly, seeing no reason to pretend she wasn't offended. "I would never do something like that and you should know me well enough to realize that."

Her mom frowned. "It was a legitimate question."

"No, it wasn't. And what is this, the Spanish Inquisition? I thought you were happy for me. That's how you sounded on the phone. Why all the questions now?"

Her dad made a point of looking around the luxurious suite and then back at Piper. She wasn't sure what that was supposed to signify, maybe more of the whole "what would a billionaire see in you except his baby" thing?

"I'm worried about you, baby." Her mom gave her that look that all mothers knew and all daughters cringed from.

"Don't be." She could not believe this. The church ceremony was in less than forty-eight hours and her parents were pulling some kind of skewed intervention. "Zee is really good to me."

"But is he good for you?" her dad asked in that old military officer-in-charge voice she'd dreaded since she was a child.

"Of course he is. How can you ask that?"

Her mom reached out and squeezed Piper's shoulder. "Money isn't everything."

"You think I am marrying him for his money? *Did you even meet him?*"

"Of course we met him. You introduced us."

"I was being sarcastic, Mom. I just can't believe you think money is the only thing Zephyr has to offer me. Or if it was, that I'd be interested. I've been taking care of myself for a long time. I've built a successful business after having my career trashed. I haven't gone through a string of loser boyfriends since Art. There's just been Zephyr and he's the most amazing man I've ever known."

How could they not see that?

"He's larger than life, that's for sure." Her mom's words agreed with Piper, but her tone was another story. "I'm just not sure that kind of man makes for a secure home."

"Oh, you mean as opposed to a husband whose career requires uprooting yourself and your children every couple of years?" Who was her mother to question Piper's choices based on that criteria, on any?

He dad got all blustery. "There's no reason to get snippy, missy. I was serving my country and well you knew it."

"Well, Zephyr serves me."

"What the hell is that supposed to mean?" her dad demanded.

"He does everything in his power to make me happy." Wasn't that obvious? It was to her. "He takes care of me, but he lets me take care of him, too. He doesn't play lord of the manor with me, but I know I can rely on him when I need him to be there for me."

"But he doesn't love you," her mother guessed in a gentle voice filled with pity.

Wow, was it a parent's job to rip their child's heart out? If it was, Piper wasn't taking that one on when this baby grew up. "Why would you say that?" she demanded in a tone far from friendly.

"Because you didn't say he did. You would have by now if it was true." The pity was still there in her mom's grey eyes.

Piper hated it. She didn't need anyone's pity. She'd chosen this marriage and she didn't regret it. She almost told them about the civil ceremony to shut them up, but she wasn't sure even that would do it. "I have what I need from him."

"You need his heart."

"That's my business."

"You're our daughter," her dad asserted. "Your happiness is our business."

"Zephyr does make me happy. Can't you see that?"

"Your dad and I think you should consider waiting to get married. At least until you get through your first trimester. I miscarried twice. What will you do if that happens to you? What happens to your marriage if the reason for that marriage doesn't come to full term?"

"That is not a scenario I am willing to discuss." She'd thought about it and decided that they would have to deal with that tragedy just like any other couple. She wasn't marrying him for the baby's sake and she didn't think he would dump her for the lack of it, either. He wanted children and one day; God willing in nine months, they would start that part of their family.

"I didn't raise you to hide from the hard stuff, Piper." Her dad's frown was softened by the very real love and concern in his eyes.

That's what she had to cling to, the knowledge that her parents loved her and were only concerned about her. They weren't trying to hurt her. "I'm not hiding."

"She's merely choosing to focus on the positive." Zephyr's voice filled Piper with relief, even as she was mortified at the thought he had overheard even part of this discussion with her parents.

Her father stood up to face Zephyr. "That's all well and good, but maybe you can answer what happens if my daughter doesn't have your baby?"

"We would deal with that tragedy like any other couple."

She couldn't help smiling at his words, which were so like her thoughts. They really were on the same wavelength.

"Some of those couples split up under the weight of the grief and *those* men and women have the benefit of love on both sides."

"I don't know about other people, but I don't give up in the face of adversity and neither does your daughter. You, of all people, should be intimately aware of that fact. She survived leaving friends and familiarity behind time and again in her childhood and a disaster of a first marriage as an adult." He put his arm out to her. "Piper isn't going to give up on our marriage, no matter what we have to face together."

She practically flew off the sofa to land against his side, the relief she felt in the shelter of his presence nearly physical. His words created another welcome layer of protection against her parents' fears and her own secret ones.

He put his arm around her waist and looked down at her as if they were the only two people in the room, as if her opinion was the only one that mattered. "You said nothing would change your feelings for me."

"It won't."

"Well, nothing will change the fact that I want you to be the mother of my children and the woman at my side, including the far-reaching possibility you will not carry this baby to term."

"Then we're golden." She smiled even as tears burned at the back of her eyes.

He set his espresso gaze on each of her parents in turn. "If that's not good enough for you, I am sorry, but I will not give your daughter up. Not now, not ever."

That was a statement of long-term intent if she'd ever heard one.

"We're not suggesting you give her up. Merely that you hold off on the wedding for a while." Piper's mom gave Zephyr her *let's be reasonable* look. "Surely, you can be a father to your child without being married to its mother."

"I can be a better father and helpmate to your daughter if we are married." Zephyr wasn't budging and she didn't think his attitude would be any different if they hadn't already been through a civil ceremony.

Piper was certain that if this discussion had come a week ago, he would have responded the same way. Unlike her parents, who were giving a very different attitude in person than they had when she called to tell them her news.

"I just don't understand," she said. "You didn't say anything about not wanting me to get married when we talked on the phone."

"This isn't something you say over a telephone line." Her mom met her eyes, willing Piper to understand.

She didn't. Not one little bit. "And you wouldn't have gotten a free trip to Greece out of it, either."

"Piper!" her mother admonished.

Her dad just frowned at her with that disappointed expression he reserved for misbehaving troops and his children.

Zephyr shook his head. "She didn't mean that." But he didn't sound disappointed in her.

He understood her parents were really hurting her and right, wrong or indifferent, she'd lashed out. "Of course I didn't. I'm sorry, but this is my time to celebrate and you're diminishing it for me."

"That is not our intention. We just want what is best for you." Her mom sounded as sincere as Piper had.

Zephyr gave her parents a considering look. "Tell me something, did you suggest she wait to marry Arthur Bellingham?"

"No," her mother answered as if she'd been forced to.

"We thought he was perfect for her," Piper's father admitted.

"That is why you are so determined to make her reconsider her decision now, isn't it? You didn't protect her from pain once and now you are going overboard to do so."

Piper had not considered that possibility. "Is that true?"

Her mom's eyes filled with tears. "We just don't want your heart broken again."

"Everyone faces pain in life, but we can't stop taking chances because of it. I trust Zee to be the husband I need. If I'm wrong, I'll deal with the fallout. What I need from you right now is not advice, but support. Can you give that to me?"

"Yes, of course," her dad said even as her mother bit her lip in worry.

But they both hugged her and apologized for hurting her feelings, if not for doubting Zephyr.

Surprisingly, dinner was relaxed and pleasant. It was as if, once having voiced their concerns, her parents gave themselves permission to simply enjoy the celebration of their daughter's second marriage. She appreciated that and did her best not to hold the discussion in her and Zephyr's suite against them.

Thankfully, her siblings' reactions were not nearly so complicated. They were thrilled for her and Zephyr, and let them both know it. They also readily admitted they thought it was beyond lovely they got a free vacation out of attending their baby sister's wedding.

Dinner with Zephyr's mother and her family was every bit as emotional as the afternoon before had been, but in a completely different way. Leda was ecstatic that her son was willing to build a relationship with her. She, too, guessed Piper was pregnant, but treated it completely as the reason for rejoicing that it was. She made it clear she was very happy Zephyr had found Piper to spend the rest of his life with and that she was looking forward to another grandchild to spoil.

His siblings were even more pleased than Piper's, his sister going so far as to offer herself as a resource for a first-time mom.

"That went well," Piper said as she dropped onto the sofa in their suite's living area after returning from the house in Kifissia.

"*Ne*…yes." Zephyr joined her on the couch, tugging her into his body and practically across his lap.

"You're such a cuddler."

"I like holding you."

"That works well for me as I like being snuggled, a lot."

"We are perfect complements to each other." He sounded very satisfied by that observation.

"We are." Even if the love only went one direction, he acted like he loved her, and in the end, wasn't it actions that mattered the most?

"Your parents are wrong," he said with absolute certainty. "This marriage is not a bad thing for either of us."

She leaned up and kissed the corner of his mouth, loving that she had the freedom to do so. "I know. And considering the fact we're already married, that's a good thing."

"Would you have listened more closely to their advice if we hadn't already gotten legally wed?"

"Seriously? You're asking me that?"

"I am."

She tilted her head to one side, considering him, and decided the time had come for a little full disclosure. "I am perfectly aware that there is a significant risk the first trimester."

"So?"

"So, I considered hashing that all out, but I didn't want to wait to marry you until we were sure. It would have felt too much like we were only getting married because I'm pregnant and while I believe that is the reason you first considered marriage, I also believe that you wouldn't tie my life to yours if you didn't want to on a level beyond that. I'm not saying you love me, but I do believe you need me." She cupped his face with both her hands. "And I *want* to be married to you."

"You are saying that you would have wanted to marry me regardless of whether or not you carried my child. The baby was a necessary catalyst to get over *my* reticence."

"Exactly." When he didn't say anything, she asked, "How do you feel about that?"

"I am surprised. Even though you said you loved me, I thought you were marrying me mostly because you are pregnant."

"Nope. I love you, and for me, that sort of goes hand in hand with me wanting to spend the rest of my life with you."

"Does it?"

She dropped her hands from his face, letting them rest against his chest, feeling his heartbeat under one palm. "Yes."

"What does it mean when a man wants to marry a woman more than he wants anything else in his life?"

Was he implying that was how he had felt? "What are you saying, Zephyr?" She couldn't afford to make assumptions about something this important.

"If your parents had convinced you to pull away from me, I would have begged you to reconsider."

"I would *never* push you away."

"That is good to hear because my experience with begging not to be left behind has not been so successful."

Suddenly, she heard exactly what he was saying and her heart filled with an aching, all-consuming love while her eyes filled with tears. "You will never have to beg me not to leave you, Zephyr. Never. I promise. I would give up anything in my life before I would give you up. My business. My reputation. My family. My friends. Anything."

"You mean that."

"Yes."

"I, too, would give up anything to be with you." There was such truth and feeling in his words, she could not breathe. "I love you, Piper."

"You don't mean that." But he did.

She could see it in every line of his face, in the dark depths of his eyes, and hear it in every word that spilled from his lips. Yet even as one part of her was doing cartwheels because he loved her, another was questioning it, doubting this happiness could truly be hers.

"Have I ever lied to you?"

"No, but you said—"

"I would have begged you to stay."

"I'm pregnant with your child."

"A wonderful bonus to be sure, but *you* are the prize, Piper Nikos. I thought my emotions had been encased in stone, but your joy in life, your inner and outer beauty, your love, they are the diamond drill bits needed to break through."

Tears slid hotly down her cheeks, but she did not rub them away. "You're getting poetic."

"Neo says that happens when you fall in love."

"I can't imagine it with him."

"You don't need to. I am the only Greek tycoon you need to be concerned with. Ever."

She wanted to laugh, but her throat was too thick with her joyful tears. "You're certainly the only man, Greek or otherwise, that I love."

"And you are the only woman I love, have ever loved or ever will love with all my heart." He kissed her, sealing the words between them like a vow.

When the kiss ended, he held her close, his hands caressing her like he was giving himself proof that she really was there. "I am sorry it took me so long to realize what I felt for you was love. I do not know how long it might have taken if

I had not overheard your parents trying to talk you out of being with me."

"You mean that conversation actually had something positive come from it?"

"If you consider me realizing I would beg you to stay if I had to and then subsequently coming to terms with what that willingness meant, then yes."

"I guess I can forgive them completely now."

He laughed and so did she.

"I can't wait to tell them you love me."

"I want to do it."

"Okay." She kissed him softly. "But tell me again, first."

And he did. Over and over, until every tiny shadow in her heart was filled with the light of their love.

Zephyr stood at the front of the church, Neo at his side, just as he had been for every life-altering moment since they met in the orphanage in Athens.

"Nervous?" Neo asked.

"Not at all. My love will walk down the aisle in just the right time."

"Did you say your *love*?"

"Ne."

"I knew you'd get your head out of your ass."

Their quiet laughter faded as the organ music heralded his bride's entrance into the sanctuary. Her mother stood and the rest of the guests—their combined families—followed suit. He knew they watched her trek up the aisle like he did, but he could not tear his gaze away from Piper for confirmation.

Her blond hair was piled on top her head in a complicated pile of curls he could not wait to muss. She wasn't wearing a veil this time, just a tiara and a radiant, glorious smile for everyone in the church to see. Her sleeveless gown whispered as one layer of taffeta moved against the other while she walked down the aisle alone.

He had not known that was her plan, but he felt the rightness of it. She offered herself to him, heart, body and soul.

The shimmering beadwork and gathered skirt with the long train on her dress *was* worthy of a modern-day royal.

"She looks like a princess," Neo observed, reflecting Zephyr's thoughts with satisfaction.

Just as Zephyr had felt contentment at Cass's beauty on his brother-by-choice's behalf.

"She is the queen of my heart."

"And you are the king of hers."

"Superman. She thinks I'm a superhero."

Neo laughed, but Zephyr ignored the quiet chuckles as Piper stopped in front of him.

He put his hand out. She took it and they turned to face the priest for a blessing on the marriage that bound the love that had made both their lives complete.

EPILOGUE

PIPER sat on a lounger on the balcony off the master bedroom of the island villa, holding her week-old baby son. He slept in the crook of her arm, oblivious to the heated discussion between his daddy and uncle about whether an American or Greek university would be the best choice for his education.

"Won't they be flabbergasted if little Erastos turns out to be an artist and wants to study at the Sorbonne?" Cass asked with laughter.

"Flabbergasted maybe, but not disappointed. Zephyr will be proud of his son, no matter what path he chooses to follow."

"And Neo? Do you think he will be proud of his child, even if he or she wants to do something flighty like play the piano or something?" Cass asked meaningfully.

"You're pregnant?" Piper demanded with joy.

The other woman had been trying since she and Neo had married, but up to now, the couple had no success. They'd been discussing visiting a fertility specialist.

Cass positively beamed. "I am."

Zephyr stopped arguing midrant and then slapped Neo on the shoulder. "You didn't tell me, you dog!"

"With any luck, we will have a daughter and she will fall as hard for your son as these special women have for us."

Zephyr looked over at Piper, his expression so filled with love it almost hurt to see it. "I can't imagine a better future for my son."

HARLEQUIN *Presents*

Coming Next Month

in **Harlequin Presents® EXTRA.** Available August 10, 2010.

#113 SWEET SURRENDER TO THE MILLIONAIRE
Helen Brooks
British Bachelors

#114 SECRETARY BY DAY, MISTRESS BY NIGHT
Maggie Cox
British Bachelors

#115 TO LOVE, HONOR AND DISOBEY
Natalie Anderson
Conveniently Wedded...& Bedded!

#116 WEDDING NIGHT WITH A STRANGER
Anna Cleary
Conveniently Wedded...& Bedded!

Coming Next Month

in **Harlequin Presents®.** Available August 31, 2010.

#2939 MARRIAGE: TO CLAIM HIS TWINS
Penny Jordan
Needed: The World's Most Eligible Billionaires

#2940 KAT AND THE DARE-DEVIL SPANIARD
Sharon Kendrick
The Balfour Brides

**#2941 THE ANDREOU MARRIAGE
ARRANGEMENT**
Helen Bianchin

**#2942 THE BILLIONAIRE'S HOUSEKEEPER
MISTRESS**
Emma Darcy
At His Service

#2943 ONE NIGHT...NINE-MONTH SCANDAL
Sarah Morgan

#2944 THE VIRGIN'S PROPOSITION
Anne McAllister

HPCNM0810

LARGER-PRINT
BOOKS!

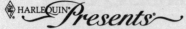

**GET 2 FREE LARGER-PRINT
NOVELS PLUS 2 FREE GIFTS!**

PASSION
GUARANTEED
SEDUCTION

YES! Please send me 2 FREE LARGER-PRINT Harlequin Presents® novels and my 2 FREE gifts (gifts are worth about $10). After receiving them, if I don't wish to receive any more books, I can return the shipping statement marked "cancel". If I don't cancel, I will receive 6 brand-new novels every month and be billed just $4.55 per book in the U.S. or $5.24 per book in Canada. That's a saving of at least 13% off the cover price! It's quite a bargain! Shipping and handling is just 50¢ per book.* I understand that accepting the 2 free books and gifts places me under no obligation to buy anything. I can always return a shipment and cancel at any time. Even if I never buy another book, the two free books and gifts are mine to keep forever.

176/376 HDN E5NG

Name	(PLEASE PRINT)	
Address		Apt. #
City	State/Prov.	Zip/Postal Code

Signature (if under 18, a parent or guardian must sign)

Mail to the **Harlequin Reader Service:**
IN U.S.A.: P.O. Box 1867, Buffalo, NY 14240-1867
IN CANADA: P.O. Box 609, Fort Erie, Ontario L2A 5X3

Not valid for current subscribers to Harlequin Presents Larger-Print books.

**Are you a subscriber to Harlequin Presents books
and want to receive the larger-print edition?
Call 1-800-873-8635 today!**

* Terms and prices subject to change without notice. Prices do not include applicable taxes. Sales tax applicable in N.Y. Canadian residents will be charged applicable provincial taxes and GST. Offer not valid in Quebec. This offer is limited to one order per household. All orders subject to approval. Credit or debit balances in a customer's account(s) may be offset by any other outstanding balance owed by or to the customer. Please allow 4 to 6 weeks for delivery. Offer available while quantities last.

HPLP10R

HARLEQUIN®

A Romance

FOR EVERY MOOD™

Spotlight on

Heart & Home

Heartwarming romances
where love can happen
right when you least expect it.

See the next page to enjoy a sneak peek
from Harlequin Superromance®,
a Heart and Home series.

Police chief Juliette Tremblant recognized the shape of the
man strolling down the street—in as calm and leisurely
fashion as if it were the middle of the day rather than
midnight. She slowed her car, convinced her eyes were
playing tricks on her. It had been a long time since Tyler
O'Neill had been seen in this town.

As she pulled to a stop at the curb, he turned toward her,
and her heart about stopped.

"What the hell are you doing here, Tyler?"

"Well, if it isn't Juliette Tremblant." He made his way
over to her, then leaned down so he could look her in the
eye. He was close enough to touch.

Juliette was not, repeat, *not* going to touch Tyler O'Neill.
Not with her fingers. Not with a ten-foot pole. There would
be no touching. Which was too bad, since it was the only
way she was ever going to convince herself the man standing
in front of her—as rumpled and heart-stoppingly handsome
now as he'd been at sixteen—was real.

And not a figment of all her furious revenge dreams.

"What are you doing back in Bonne Terre?" she asked.

"The manor is sitting empty," Tyler said and shrugged,
as though his arriving out of the blue after ten years was
casual. "Seems like someone should be watching over the
family home."

"You?" She laughed at the very notion of him being here
for any unselfish reason. "Please."

He stared at her for a second, then smiled. Her heart fluttered against her chest—a small mechanical bird powered by that smile.

"You're right." But that cryptic comment was all he offered.

Juliette bit her lip against the other questions.

Why did you go?

Why didn't you write? Call?

What did I do?

But what would be the point? Ten years of silence were all the answer she really needed.

She had sworn off feeling anything for this man long ago. Yet one look at him and all the old hurt and rage resurfaced as though they'd been waiting for the chance. That made her mad.

She put the car in gear, determined not to waste another minute thinking about Tyler O'Neill. "Have a good night, Tyler," she said, liking all the cool "go screw yourself" she managed to fit into those words.

It seems Juliette has an old score to settle with Tyler.
Pick up TYLER O'NEILL'S REDEMPTION
to see how he makes it up to her.
Available September 2010,
only from Harlequin Superromance.